IT WAS LIKE LISTENING TO A FAUCET DRIPPING WITH BLOOD

First a man rich in worldly goods was blown to bits when his expensive auto exploded.

Then a saintly man of God met his Maker when he was crucified to the floor of his church, with barbed wire forming a bloody crown on his head.

Next a young man as innocent as a child was done to death in a manner calculated to make the most hardened adult sick to his stomach.

Who would be next? The New York City ex-detective who found himself in the middle of this nightmare? The beautiful young girl who used his bed and his embrace as a haven from horror? The ponderous local police chief who swore vengeance?

Every person in town looked at each other and wondered if he saw a killer—and in the mirror and wondered if he saw a future victim. . . .

Also by William E. Chambers

The Redemption Factor

DEATH TOLL

A novel by William E. Chambers

Mystery Writers of America Presents
New York   Lincoln   Shanghai

Death Toll

Mystery Writers of America Presents
an imprint of iUniverse, Inc.

For information address:
iUniverse
2021 Pine Lake Road, Suite 100
Lincoln, NE 68512
www.iuniverse.com

Originally published by Popular Library

ISBN: 0-595-20056-7

Printed in the United States of America

For my Marie, naturally . . .

Chapter One

It was a great feeling to open my eyes and not see Amanda's discontented puss. The real thrill came from knowing her lack of presence was permanent. I rolled out of bed, slipped into a pair of cut-away denims, and stepped out onto my sagging porch. My bungalow might not have pleased Amanda or the queen of England, but it faced the ocean and was separated from neighboring dwellings by an eighth of a mile of sand in each direction. It had three rooms, a shower, and the rent was reasonable. What more could I want?

It was unusually warm for mid-May, so I sprinted through the sand into the surf and leaped at the first respectable breaker that appeared. The icy wave shocked the drowsiness out of me. I thrashed about, revving my circulation, then heeded the rumbling in my stomach and headed back to the bungalow. A cold shower and hot breakfast readied me for the task ahead.

I cleared the dishes, set my typewriter and paper up on the table, and put my index and middle fingers to work. Four hours and three pages later, I felt I deserved a drink. The question was, Should I make it myself or explore Paradise Village's pub scene? Being curious by nature, I decided to search. Since I was in need of exercise, I chose my English racer over my Oldsmobile. With my pocket transistor tuned in to soft music, I pedaled down the narrow tar road that separated the high sand dunes.

I hummed to the music until it was interrupted by a news broadcast. National problems aside, the most exciting local story revolved around a high school break-in. The crime seemed pointless since, except for a jimmied window, nothing had been damaged or stolen. This was a far cry from the headlines in New York City. It was comforting to know that there were still some civilized areas left in the world.

Civilized and deserted. For the first fifteen minutes of my journey, I had the sunshine, salt air, and seagulls to myself. The houses I passed were still and there weren't any swimmers or fishermen to be seen. Probably because it was still too early in the season.

The first people I saw were at Doddard's Body and Fender Shop, located on the edge of town. Inside the opened garage stood a mechanic in grease-stained coveralls. Outside, climbing into a polished black Jaguar, was a plump, middle-aged man. Both men waved to me and I waved back. It was nice to find a town where even the strangers were friendly.

The Jaguar purred into life as I passed by. This sound was followed by a deafening roar and a blast of heat that wrenched me from my bike. I landed on my back in a sandbank and realized, after a couple of blinks, that I was looking up at my feet. I shifted about till I was right side up, then caught my breath. Flames enveloped the Jaguar. Its windows had fragmented, littering the road with glass slivers. A charred, inhuman-looking figure slumped against the steering wheel. The mechanic was fanning the flames with his shirt in a desperate attempt to reach the front door. I ran across the road, jerked him backwards by the arm, and said, "Too late for that. Who is he?"

"Sam Doddard. M—my boss."

Grease spots aside, his complexion resembled white marble. Getting him away from the scene seemed like a good idea, so I said, "Where's your phone?"

"In the office."

"Show me."

He led me into the office and pointed to the phone on the desk, then staggered past a row of file cabinets to a door marked TOILET. Sounds of his retching filled the room as I dialed the operator and asked for the police. Three rings passed before a voice said, "Sheriff Bodin's office. Sheriff Bodin speaking."

"My name is Callahan, Sheriff. A car exploded outside of Doddard's garage. Sam Doddard was killed—"

"Exploded? Sam killed?"

"Yes. Get the fire engines out here right—"

"What did you say your name was?"

"Callahan! Listen! Just get—"

"Is this some sort of prank?"

"Goddamn it! There's been an explosion out here—"

"Callahan, eh? There's only two men in this

7

town with that name, and you don't sound like either one of them—"

"Listen, you stupid bastard—"

"Now see here! I'm the sheriff, you know. You can't—"

"Then act like the sheriff and get your ass out here!"

I slammed the phone down so hard I cracked the receiver. Whistles that were undoubtedly signals for the volunteer fire department filled the air. My friend stopped retching. He walked shakily to the desk and flopped down in the revolving chair behind it. Now, with some of the grease removed from his face, he looked about seventeen. I said, "Any whiskey around here?"

"Top drawer. First cabinet."

I found a bottle of Scotch and poured him some in a paper cup. He shook his head, saying, "I don't drink."

"This is a good time to start."

While he struggled with the Scotch, I watched the sheriff's black-and-gray car arrive, followed by two fire trucks. The firemen immediately went into action, dousing the flames with white foam. First man out of the police car was the driver. His companion, who was stout, to put it mildly, found exiting a little more difficult. I figured he was my man. As he shook his head at the burning car and attempted to straighten out his ill-fitting uniform, I approached him and said, "Sheriff?"

A pink face with blue eyes turned to me. "Yes?"

"I'm Marty Callahan."

"Callahan! So you're—" The sheriff's voice trailed off as he studied my face more closely. "I

8

recognize you. Lieutenant Marty Callahan! From New York City!"

"Ex-lieutenant. Retired."

"You don't say. Did you—" Bodin pointed to the car. "Did you see what happened?"

"Not exactly. Luckily I had just passed when it exploded. That's my bike over there in the sand."

"The back wheel's bent out of shape."

"One second sooner and I would have been bent out of shape."

"What could have caused such an explosion, do you think?"

"I'd say a bomb."

"Bomb!" Bodin looked horrified. "Sam Doddard didn't have an enemy in the world."

"Then his friends have a queer sense of humor."

A van bearing the lettering of the town's local TV station parked directly across the street from us. Two conservatively dressed men, one carrying a portable tape recorder, the other a portable movie camera, forged their way through the growing crowd. The tape wielder damn near thrust his mike into the sheriff's mouth and said, "What happened, Abner?"

Bodin waited until he was sure the cameraman had him focused in properly, then said, "It looks like murder, boys."

"Murder?" They sounded like a duet.

"A bomb." Bodin's eyes flicked in my direction. "But I can't say so definite. Have to wait until the state police arrive with their bomb expert, seein' as how we don't have one of our own."

"Will the state police be handling this case, Abner?"

Bodin's barrel chest expanded menacingly as he

9

glared at his questioner. "Of course not! Except for certain technical areas, the case is totally under my jurisdiction and I'll handle it."

"But Abner, you've never had a murder on your hands before."

The look on Bodin's face told me that a second murder might be on his hands before the questioning was over. However, the sheriff contained his anger and answered in measured tones: "I am a trained police officer with a small but competent staff. I have also been fortunate enough to befriend a fellow officer from New York City whose vast knowledge and experience in crime fighting is at my disposal."

I had started to edge into the crowd when a hand covered my shoulder and collarbone. Bodin said, "Allow me to introduce Lieutenant Marty Callahan."

The camera swung toward me. The reporter said, "Are you the same Lieutenant Callahan who broke the Turkish narcotics ring in New York a few months ago?"

He knew I was the same Callahan, but for Paradise Village, this was good TV fare. I said, "Yes."

"What do you think of the murder?"

"I have no opinion. I'm just down here on vaca—"

Bodin grabbed the reporter's wrist, swung the mike away from me, and spoke into it himself. "Mr. Callahan prefers to keep an open mind and suspend judgment until all the facts are known."

The mike was too far away to pick up my "I do?"

One of Bodin's deputies chalked the position of the car on the ground while Bodin snapped photographs from various angles. Since the news camera was following him, he spent a lot of time adjusting the settings and shooting the pictures. Having come to Paradise to write mysteries, and not solve them, I decided now was a good time to slip away from the scene. As I did, I wondered if Bodin had remembered to load his camera with film.

I was sitting in Bodin's office, trying unsuccessfully to repair my damaged transistor radio, when he returned. I said, "Door was open. Let myself in."

"Good. I need a formal statement from you."

"I figured that. So here I am."

"Fine. Come inside."

A row of uncomfortable wood folding chairs lined each wall in the outer office and I was glad to leave mine. Bodin opened the knee-high gate and ushered me into his antiseptic green office with his free hand. Two gray metal desks, a table with a two-way radio, and a couple of file cabinets were the main contents of the room. A large map of Paradise Village and a dart board adorned one wall. The dart board looked well used. I said, "Where's the rest of your force?"

"Two of my men are off duty and the other two took the mechanic to the hospital. Speaking of hospitals, you should get checked up yourself."

I waved that away. "The sand was soft."

"Still—"

"Don't worry. I'm O.K. Did anyone inform Doddard's relatives?"

"Uh—" Bodin loosened his necktie and glanced about self-consciously. "The—uh—mayor thought

11

I should tell Violet—Mrs. Doddard—but Dick—uh—volunteered to do it after he dropped me off. Now let's—get this business over with."

Bodin typed my statement as efficiently as any secretary, and I signed it. I said, "Wish I could type like that."

"Really?" His face flushed with pleasure. "It takes lots of practice."

"I keep promising myself I'm going to learn, but I never seem to get around to it."

"Why do you want to learn typing?"

"Because I write mysteries as a hobby."

"No kidding? Ever been published?"

"Couple of short stories. Nothing big. Never had time to do it seriously before."

"Well, if you need a typist, I can get you one. Most of the kids around here learn it in school."

"Good to know. I finished a couple of stories while recuperating from my last case."

"I read where you had been shot."

"I caught one in the chest. Lousy gunman. He was aiming for my head."

"That's the fella you shot through the heart?"

"Yeah. I was aiming for his balls."

"You were—Mr. Callahan!"

We both laughed until Bodin said, "Shame about your partner, though."

"Yeah."

"And the way the case ended up. I mean, it wasn't your fault. You can't blame yourself—"

"I'd rather not discuss it." I stood up and said, "Anything else?"

"I—uh"—Bodin nervously patted his dozen strands of gray hair—"I'll have to hold your bike

12

as evidence. I snapped some pictures of it in the sand, but I think I better . . ."

"No problem. That it?"

"Yes."

"Good-bye."

Chapter Two

The next morning the sea breeze was cool, the sun bright, and my typewriter hot. The paragraphs just flowed onto the paper as I worked before the opened kitchen window. By noon I had accomplished more than I expected to, so I decided to reward myself. I popped open a can of beer, but before I could taste it, I heard a light tapping at my door. I walked into the living room and opened it. A ravishing doe-eyed redhead who couldn't have been more than twenty smiled at me. I said, "Whatever you're selling, I'll take some."

"Hello, Mr. Callahan. I'm Robin Blair."

"Lovely name. You certainly deserve it."

"Why, thank you."

"Thank Mother Nature. I'm just an observer. What can I do for you?"

"Sheriff Bodin said you could use a typist."

"So I can. Come in."

I studied her walk as I closed the door. It had to be natural. You just couldn't fake something like that. Though blue jeans and a black windbreaker are not especially noted for enhancing the female form, they couldn't hide her gifts. I said, "What are your rates?"

"Quarter a page. Ten cents for carbons."

"That's a bargain. Want a beer?"

"No, thanks. Too early for beer."

"Whiskey, then?"

Amusement widened her sparkling green eyes. "You're teasing me."

"I never joke about religion or alcohol. Sit down. I'll get the manuscripts."

It took about a minute to fish them out of the dresser drawer in my bedroom. As I handed them to Robin, another knock came to the door. This time it sounded like a maniac with a sledgehammer. I said, "Excuse me. I think the building's being condemned."

I opened the door, and a very round boy in a denim tent said, "Hi!"

"Hi!"

"I'm Herbie Dorfus. Are you Callahan, the famous detective?"

"No. I'm Irving the astronaut."

"You're Callahan. I saw you on TV. Gonna help out with the case, huh?"

"No. I'm gonna help out with the case."

"The sheriff's been telling everybody about your dope bust and how he can count on your help."

"I wish he had told me. Now, what can I do for you?"

"Can I have your autograph? If you solve this case, I want everybody to know that I know you."

He handed me a grade school graduate's autograph book and I signed it. After he left, I said, "That kid's thick. And I don't mean his body."

"You really aren't going to help with the case?" Robin looked surprised. "The sheriff's been giving the impression . . ."

"He's great at impressions."

"Oh, well." She sounded disappointed. "How many copies do you want?"

"I want each story freshly typed with one carbon."

"I'll have them for you as soon as I can."

"Fine."

" 'Bye."

" 'Bye."

Robin's departure heightened my concentration —not on my story, on Robin. Since I had finished my stint anyway, I decided it was time for a diversion. Maybe now I could check out the pub scene.

I explored the town through the windshield of my car. Most of the houses were high, gabled, and pre-Civil War vintage. Elm trees shaded the streets. The town square was lined with park benches, stores, and cafés. Since it wasn't yet tourist time, not all the businesses had been opened.

Globed streetlights, resembling gaslights of old, were arranged around the square. A magnificent view of the ocean was available from here, although a few houses and the rambling frame of Town Hall dotted the scene. In the distance beyond Town Hall I noticed a lighthouse. I decided to check it out.

I was delighted to discover that the lighthouse had been converted into a tavern. Nautical supplies such as ship's helms, fishnets, and anchors decorated the walls and ceiling. Sawdust was sprinkled across the floor, and soft music filled the room. I sat at the end of the bar so I could watch through the windows as the ocean's waves thrashed the rocks outside. Several old-timers lounged about, sipping beer and speaking in undertones. I ordered a beer myself, drank it, and ordered another. I was halfway through my refill when a rather unkempt-looking male entered. He straddled a stool and said, "Large beer, Adolph."

I looked at the balding, hunchbacked bartender, who answered in what might have been his sister's voice, "Get lost, Charley, you frigging thing."

Charley waved a dollar bill like it was Old Glory. "I got money and I want a beer."

Adolph produced a lead-and-leather blackjack from beneath the bar and said, "Don't make me smash you."

Retired or not, my police instinct was aroused. I said, "Hey, Adolph! You've proved you're worthy of your name. Now put the sap down."

Adolph's weasel-like face turned toward me. The cop in me must have shown through because as soon as our eyes met he shelved the weapon. I said, "You can do time for threatening people like that."

Adolph's wrists went limp with disgust. He said, "Whenever Charley has a dollar, he thinks he's so special."

Adolph reluctantly poured a beer, which Charley accepted, saying, "See that you give me the right change."

Charley strolled over and sat on the stool beside me. The smell about him could never be bottled or marketed. He said, "I'm Charley Fetters. Ain't you Marty Callahan, the detective?"

"I'm Marty Callahan, but I'm no longer—"

"Sure. I seen you on TV." He turned to the men

at the bar, jiggled a thumb an inch or two in front of my nose, and shouted, "Hey, clowns! His honor here is an honest-to-goodness detective from New York City, not a bag of guts like fat-ass Bodin."

"You really have a nice thumb, Charley," I remarked, "but when you've seen one, you've seen 'em all."

"What? Oh! Sorry."

He withdrew his hand. I was wishing he'd withdraw his body. The old-timers were imprisoning me with looks when a noisy mob of guys and gals stormed through the door, diverting attention away from me. They monopolized the front end and kept Adolph busy. Charley took a swig of beer and said, "Figured out who did it yet?"

"Did what?"

"Killed old Doddard."

I took a deep breath, let it out slowly, and said, "I am not working on or even interested in this murder case. Please dismiss any notions to the contrary from your mind."

Annoyance must have made me raise my voice because someone at the front of the bar overheard my statement and asked, "What's the matter, Callahan? This case too tough for a New York pro like you?"

I glanced over at a muscular young man wearing a white windbreaker and black jeans. He seemed a bit taller than my own six feet, had long blond hair, and was deeply tanned. Charley muttered, "That's Burton Hanlon, the mayor's son. Thinks he owns the town."

Adolph said, "He does, practically."

All the members of the young set were silent. They seemed eager to hear my reply. I didn't give

18

them any. I just turned to Charley and made some inconsequential remark or other. The bartender shuffled over with two beers and said, "On the mayor's son."

Hanlon's voice rang out again. "Hey, Callahan, I hope you're not so much of a celebrity that you can't have a drink on me."

I glanced at the beer but didn't touch it. Charley started to reach for his, but I dissuaded him with a slight shake of the head. Looking at Hanlon, I said, "I don't think a short appearance on your local TV really makes me a celebrity."

He laughed and said, "I wasn't referring to the TV."

"What were you referring to? My drug bust?"

"No."

"What, then?"

Hanlon pointed his finger at Charley and said, "The glorious company you keep."

Hanlon's whole crowd convulsed with laughter. I waited until the noise died down, then said, "I appreciate your reasoning. I am fussy who I associate with."

Slowly, deliberately, I picked up both beer mugs, reached across the bar to the drainage section, and dumped the drinks. The room fell so silent you could hear your own breathing. Hanlon's cheekbones whitened and his lips compressed. A freckle-faced girl occupying the stool beside him fluttered her eyelashes from him to me, then back to him again. None of his friends spoke or moved. Suddenly he flashed a smile and said, "I should have expected that. Birds of a feather, you know."

Again the crowd roared with laughter, and nor-

19

malcy resumed. I bought another round for Charley and myself and glanced up at the TV, which was located near the ceiling at the back of the room. Adolph had flicked the remote-control unit to catch the news. The announcer asserted that the state police had proved the car was booby-trapped. Then the picture flashed back to yesterday's bomb scene and there I was. I looked pretty good on camera. Or maybe it just seemed that way because Bodin looked so gross. Whatever the reason, if I had been a little less impressed with myself, I might have avoided experiencing the explosion that occurred inside my brain.

The first sight to greet my bloodshot eyes was a pair of bloodshot eyes. They belonged to a cat who looked like a breathing X ray. He belched in my face. Right then I realized I was lying down and he was using my chest as a pillow. I said, "Pussycat, you have no manners."

Somewhere behind me I heard Charley say, "Obnoxious! Get off the nice man's chest. Shame on you."

Obnoxious's only response was to roll his irritated eyes toward Charley. I did the same. Charley, who had one hand behind his back, said, "Watch this!"

He brought his hand around. It contained a can of beer. The cat sprang up and down on my chest like it was a trampoline. Then, imitating a police siren, he leaped onto the floor and charged toward a saucer in a corner of the room. Charley winked at me and said, "Catch this operation."

He half filled the saucer with beer and explained, "Had the habit when I inherited him

20

from a friend who slipped into the Great Beyond. That's why my friend named him Obnoxious. I tried to cure him, but take the sauce away and he goes bananas. So I have to deliver his quota."

I put a hand on my face, felt a tumor where my cheek should be, and reminded myself that I was supposed to be standing or sitting at the Lighthouse's bar admiring my TV image and not lying on a fold-out sofa bed in a one-room hovel. I said, "Charley, what the hell happened?"

"So!" Charley's face assumed the coy expression of a child who knows a secret but is in no hurry to tell. "You don't remember anything, eh?"

"Sure I remember. I'm just asking questions to exercise my tongue."

"Hanlon suckered you sweet, he did. You was leanin' sideways against the bar, lookin' up at the TV, and he sneaked up behind you and threw a left hook over your shoulder. You hit the deck like a drunken sailor."

I sat up slowly as Charley continued, "Young Hanlon doesn't like to be outdone. Used to his own way, he is."

"How did I get here?"

"Me and some of the guys brought you over. Couldn't leave you layin' on the floor."

"'Course not. I might have tripped somebody. This your place?"

"I stay here in return for helpin' Mrs. Bridges. She rents cabins and I clean and do repairs for her, you know?"

I staggered over to the window, pushed the cobwebbed curtains aside, and opened it. The cool salt air eased my throbbing head.

"How far is this place from the bar?"

"Three-quarters of a block."

"Hanlon still there?"

"Nope. Him and his friends took their bikes and beat it right after he blitzed you."

I examined the welt on my cheek through the cracked mirror above Charley's sink and said, "This has been some vacation."

Chapter Three

I felt pretty good the next morning in spite of the fact that one side of my face had outgrown the other. I swam, showered, and cooked sausages, toast, and eggs. The fried yolks reminded me of Charley's cat's eyes. I washed breakfast down with hot coffee and got set for my daily battle with the typewriter. I had just inserted the paper when a knock came to the door. I shouted, "Come in. The door's open."

Robin entered wearing shorts and a halter that made yesterday's outfit seem like a nun's habit. She smiled, waved a manila envelope, and said, "Hi! Here's your cop—your face!"

"Sure it's my face. Don't let anyone tell you otherwise."

She reached out and gently touched my bruise. It didn't hurt, but I flinched anyway. She withdrew her fingers and said, "I'm sorry! How did it happen?"

Robin's face reddened as I explained. She said, "That bum!"

"Careful, now. Your sunburn's showing."

"Sunburn?"

"If that's not sunburn, you must be crazy about me."

"I've—uh—I've finished your copies."

"That was fast."

"No sense wasting time."

"Pretty and practical. My kind of girl."

"Oh? Really?"

"Yep. My wife had the first quality but not the second."

"Oh! You're married?"

"Divorced. Feel free to make advances."

"Ha! You are something."

"I take that as a compliment. What do I owe you?"

"Ten dollars and fifty cents."

"Let's settle at a round figure. Ten dollars and I take you to dinner."

Robin's smile almost blinded me. "When?"

"Well, since you can't eat dinner until dinnertime, how about tonight?"

"Fine."

"I don't know my way around, so you'll have to choose the restaurant."

"O.K."

"Someplace with atmosphere and good steaks."

"I know just the—oh!"

"What?"

"I just remembered. I'm going to Mr. Doddard's wake tonight."

"How about afterwards?"

"O.K. Unless . . ."

"Yes?"

"Would you care to accompany me? We could go out right afterwards."

"I don't relish wakes, but . . . why not?"

24

"Great."

"What time shall I pick you up?"

"Sevenish?"

"Fine."

She gave me her address, explaining it was just down the road a piece. That last word stuck in my mind as I watched her mount her bike and pedal away.

"Seven sharp," I said.

"Come in. I like a man who's on time."

Robin was stunning in a plain, knee-length black dress as she greeted me at the door. Her house was a cozy four room affair with an over-sized fireplace in the living room and a menacing-looking bear rug on the floor. I looked around appraisingly and said, "Beautiful. Just beautiful."

"So! You like my place."

"Silly, I'm talking about you. I never even noticed the place."

She smiled and said, "You're silly."

"Weddings and wakes always lighten my mood."

"Marty! Shame on you!"

"I apologize meekly and humbly."

"Would you like something before we leave?"

"What did you have in mind?"

"I meant to drink."

"Never touch the stuff."

"Oh, let's go."

Sam Doddard, having been a wealthy man with a house that could accommodate far more people than the town's solitary funeral parlor, was laid out at home in a closed bronze casket. The Doddard home was a high-gabled mansion that perched on the crest of a carefully landscaped hill. We entered this property by driving through opened wrought-iron gates that were fastened to the rock-and-mortar walls surrounding the land. There was still enough sunlight left to give us a good view of the estate. Two tennis courts and a kidney-shaped swimming pool passed my line of vision before we reached the house. I said, "Looks like Doddard did all right financially."

"Oh, yes. He owned a chain of garages in several different cities. The one in town was just a hobby."

"Really?"

"Sure. A lot of people in this town made their money elsewhere and came here to relax and play. But tourists began to drift in, and when they couldn't scare them or chase them away, they decided to profit from them."

"I guess that makes sense."

I thought I detected an edge in her tone when she said, "They've made concessions, but they still control."

Coasting to a halt behind a line of cars, I was about to ask just who the mysterious *they* were when a uniformed butler approached. He peered into my opened window and said, "Good evening, sir, madam."

We responded to the greeting and followed him into the house. Doddard's home could easily have been a comfortable museum. Grecian statues, flowing fountains, and Persian rugs softer than foam-rubber innersoles were what impressed me the most. However, the crystal chandeliers and original paintings didn't escape my observation either. Especially the nudes. My mind was spinning with thoughts totally unrelated to, and improper for, a wake when I entered the room with the mourners.

The casket, which was closed, of course, was made of bronze and situated in the center of a round room. Candles flickered on top of tall gold stands at the head and foot of it. Rows of folding chairs were set in wide circles around the room. Nearly every one was filled. Robin and I marched self-consciously to the casket, knelt before it, and said a prayer. Then, following her lead, I joined the line that formed to pay respects to the widow.

Mrs. Doddard was a tall, slim brunette. Although in her early forties, she appeared ten years younger. Robin greeted her and introduced me. When I expressed my condolences, she clasped my hand with a grip that was surprisingly firm and said, "Thank you, Mr. Callahan. And thank you for your kind offer to help with this invest—" Her voice broke.

I said, "There's no need to thank me."

She did again, anyway, then turned to greet the people waiting behind me. A gleam brightened Robin's eyes as she led me to a chair. She said, "I knew you'd help out."

"I didn't promise anything."

"You didn't deny anything, either."

"I was put on the spot. Taken unawares."

"You've got a heart of gold."

"With a lead lining."

Robin suppressed a smile while I studied the faces of the mourners. I saw the fat kid who nearly pounded my door in hunting for an autograph. He was sitting next to an older but otherwise exact duplicate. I said, "There's Herbie, before and after."

Robin chuckled, then explained, "That's his father. He's principal of Paradise Village High School. Herbie's a freshman. Smartest kid in his class."

"Could be an un-kosher connection there."

"You're too suspicious."

"'Suspect everyone' is the policeman's creed. Uh-oh!"

Robin's eyes followed my line of vision and rested upon the figure of the man who had temporarily altered the shape of my face. Burton Hanlon wore an expensive, carefully tailored black suit. Next to him stood a short man with pearl-white hair and an ivory complexion. He was also expensively dressed and was talking to the widow. Robin said, "That's Mayor Hanlon."

"I figured as much."

"Because he was with Burton?"

"No. Because his mouth hasn't stopped moving since I laid eyes on him. Sure sign of a politician."

Robin didn't seem amused. She said, "That's just one way. There are others."

The mayor and his son sat beside the widow. Two clergymen were next on line. Robin said, "The tall, skinny man is Father Moore. He's our only Catholic priest except for during the tourist months when he receives some outside help. The little, bald one is a minister. Reverend Tyson. They're our only resident clergymen."

"Seem to be good friends."

"They have a lot in common."

"I hope you aren't referring to the collection plate."

28

"Marty! You are terrible."

"That's what makes me so charming."

"We have company." Robin's voice hardened. I looked up and saw the mayor and his son approaching. His Honor nodded somberly to most of the mourners and smiled sadly at some others. He stopped before us, extended a soft white hand to me, and said, "Good evening, Miss Blair, Mr. Callahan. I'm Mayor Hanlon, sir. Please don't rise."

I don't know what made him think I was going to stand up. I just shifted position because sitting too still activates my hemorrhoids. I said, "Hello."

"This is my son, Burton."

Burton grunted. I accepted his reluctantly offered hand and squeezed it till he grimaced. The mayor said, "I wish to extend the gratitude of the mayor's office and the people of Paradise Village for the helping hand you've so graciously offered in this, our time of need."

I yawned. He pretended not to notice but dropped the speech and said, "What happened to your cheek?"

"Something slimy touched it." I smiled at his granite-faced son. The mayor buffed the neatly manicured nails of his right hand against his jacket and said, "Well—very nice to have met you. Good night."

As the mayor turned to shake hands with other mourners, Burton threw a hard-boiled look in my direction, then rejoined his father. Robin said, "We've paid our respects. I think we can go now."

We made one more trip to the casket, again extended our condolences to the widow, and left. Once outside, I asked, "Where to, Bru-tay?"

"Town square."

Robin stared moodily through the windshield as I drove to town. After several attempts at conversation failed, I asked, "Who don't you like? The mayor or his son?"

"Both."

"How come?"

"Let's not talk about it."

"What do you want to talk about?"

"Nothing."

"Fascinating subject. Bet the mayor could converse about it for hours."

Robin's lips turned slightly upward. I continued, "Why, I bet your mayor's head is filled with that subject. A family gift he can pass through his genes to posterity."

Robin laughed. "He already has."

Seeing the town square was like stepping a hundred years into the past. The streetlights glowed like huge pearls, and people strolled leisurely about or relaxed on the wood benches. High hats and hoopskirts wouldn't have been out of place here.

The restaurant Robin picked was called King Richard's Rib House and was cavelike in atmosphere. Thick oak beams crisscrossed the high ceilings. Electric lights in the shape of candles burned from round wood chandeliers attached to these beams by heavy black chains. Logs crackled and burned in a massive stone fireplace that was guarded on either side by a suit of armor. Music was provided by flute-playing court jesters while Maid Marian herself guided us to a round oak table. I drank ale in pewter tankards while Robin

sipped coffee. We both ate succulent steaks. I said,
"Your name's perfect for this place."

"My name?"

"Robin. As in Robin Hood?"

"You're right. Very clever."

"I'm educated. Eight years of high school."

"You're delightful." She reached over and
touched my hand. I felt a twinge of pleasure. But
not in my hand. "Let's go back to my house. I can
get a fire going, too."

I wouldn't have touched that line for all the
ribs in King Richard's House.

I had forgotten about the bear rug and almost
had a stroke when Robin turned on the light.
"Some pet you've got there."

"He guards my liquor. What would you like?"

"Dangerous question."

"To drink, I mean."

"A Scotch and soda would be soothing."

"I'll get the Scotch. You get the soda."

"Where?"

"There's a case of bottles out in the garage."

Robin opened a closet in the foyer between the
living room and bedroom. She pulled a cord and
the closet lit, revealing an array of unopened bottles. I said, "How do I get into the garage? From
outside?"

She pointed to a door between the living room
and kitchen. This led to the basement, which led,
in turn, to the garage. A decidedly masculine influence reigned in here. Tools were mounted on
the walls. An archery set stood in one corner of
the room alongside several cases of soda. But most
peculiar was the ten-year-old Pontiac Bonneville

31

with a mashed-in front, cracked windshield, and four flat tires that monopolized most of the room. Even the gas cap was missing. I scooped up a bottle of club soda, returned to the kitchen, and said, "What's with the old wreck in the garage?"

Robin hesitated, then said, "It's—it used to be my father's car. He took great pride in it. After he died I couldn't part with it. Keeping it was like having part of him close by."

"But it's wrecked. How'd that happen?"

"Accident. That's how he died."

"Oh. Have you got a crowbar?"

"Crowbar?"

"I want to pry my foot out of my mouth."

Robin laughed, handed me a drink, and said, "Forget it. Let's go inside."

We reentered the living room and settled on the overstuffed sofa. Robin had gotten a fire going while I was in the garage. She said, "Bottoms up."

I let my eyes wander over her, then said, "Not a bad idea."

We clicked glasses and drank. My Scotch went down nice and smooth. Robin's eyes tightened and her nose wrinkled. She spent several seconds like this, then opened her eyes and said, "Ah! That was good."

I slipped my arm around her and drew her head to my chest. We kissed. She smiled. We drank. She frowned. "Robin, are you sure you like Scotch?"

"Mmm. My favorite drink. What I like about Scotch is that it's tough going down, but once there, settles nicely."

"I've never experienced the former effect. Only the latter."

I watched over the rim of my glass as her face tightened. She looked like a reluctant diver about to plunge. But she drank. A rosy glow tinged her skin and lights burned brightly in her eyes as she rattled the ice in her empty glass.

"Ready for another, Marty?"

"Marty's ready for anything."

Robin's walk seemed a bit unsteady as she returned to the kitchen. I shrugged, thumbed my nose at the bear, and settled back to enjoy the warmth surging through me. Robin came back with refills. She braced her face and we drank. I put my arm back into position, nibbled on her ear, and whispered, "You're very lovely."

"And you're very nice. It was really good of you to offer your services to Mrs. Doddard."

I was about to restate my disinterest in the whole affair when I realized such a comment might shatter the mood of the evening. Instead, I said, "I'm good at servicing."

"I'll bet you are."

She took my drink and placed it beside her own on the lamp table next to the sofa. Our arms entwined and our lips fused. I picked her up and carried her into the bedroom, where the sounds of night, waves gently lapping the shore, a seagull cawing in the distance, were replaced by tender whispers, passionate whimpers, and blissful oblivion.

Chapter Four

When I first opened my eyes, I didn't know where I was. I glanced about the cedar-paneled bedroom and gradually recalled the events of the previous evening. The aroma of fresh coffee and the sizzling of bacon told me all was right with the world. Robin appeared in the doorway, wearing a cotton robe. She smiled and said, "Get dressed, sleepyhead. Breakfast is almost ready."

"What I'm hungry for, you can't stick in a toaster."

"Later. Rise and shine."

She disappeared from the doorway, so I staggered into the bathroom. A quick hot-cold shower sharpened my appetite. Dressed in a towel, I entered the kitchen looking like a run-down Tarzan. Scrambled eggs, bacon, sausage, toast, and coffee awaited my pleasure. Robin said, "I want to make sure you keep your strength up."

I slipped into the chair facing hers, flicked on the radio that was plugged in next to the toaster, and said, "Sounds like you have plans for me."

She twitched her nose like a rabbit. Soft music played as I devoured food and coffee. A burp escaped me when I wiped my lips with a napkin.

Before I could excuse myself, Robin said, "I graciously accept your compliment."

"Shall I repeat it?"

"Once is enough. Don't bring it up again."

"Have you got an extra toothbrush?"

"In the bathroom."

I brushed my teeth while Robin cleared the table. Then I sat on the sofa and waited while she did the same. An impish smile crossed her face as she reentered the room and said, "Aren't you going to put on your clothes?"

"What for? I'll only have to take them off again."

"You're right." She undid the belt of her robe and said, "This is no time for formalities."

As though on cue, the music stopped and a strong voice declared, "Bulletin! Bulletin! Bulletin! The Paradise Village Broadcasting Network received a letter in the mail today concerning the motive behind the murder of one of our most noted citizens, Samuel Doddard."

Robin turned sharply toward the radio. Mixed emotions of curiosity and frustration warred within me. Curiosity won. I listened attentively as the broadcaster read the contents of the letter.

" 'Fellow citizens and potential victims, I greet you. Paradise Village is, aside from tourist months, populated by approximately two thousand prosperous citizens. For the nominal sum of one hundred twenty-five dollars apiece, a total of two hundred and fifty thousand dollars, tragedies such as Sam Doddard's demise can be prevented. Details of how to collect and deliver this tax, or—if you will—Death Toll, shall be furnished in the near future. Meantime, reflect upon the loss of your esteemed Mr. Doddard. You have more in common with him than you know.' "

The broadcaster went on to announce that Sheriff Bodin was working on this latest development. Satisfied that the situation was well in hand, my own two hands took up where they had left off. But Robin was no longer receptive. She closed her robe and said, "Aren't you going over to see Sheriff Bodin?"

"What for?"

"He may need your help."

"I'm sure I can accomplish a lot more right here."

"Stop being silly. This is serious."

"I'm being serious. I can't do anything."

Robin folded her arms, exhaled indignantly, and said, "At least you could try."

"O.K. O.K. I'll try."

Ten minutes later I was dressed and ready to leave. So was Robin. She said, "I'm going with you, O.K.?"

"Fine. It'll make it easier for me to eat my heart out."

Bodin's face was red and shiny when we entered his office. He sat behind his desk holding a phone to his ear with one hand and a handkerchief with the other. He waved and motioned us to sit down. We took seats and waited as he sputtered into the phone. "Yes, sir. We're doing the best we can. No—no state police. Not yet, anyway. Yes, sir. Mr. Callahan just came in. He'll help out." He winked at me. "Yes, sir. 'Bye, sir."

Bodin hung up, shook his head, and whistled. "That was the mayor. Wanted to know what I'm doing about the note. The press bugged the hell out of me all morning. What the hell does everyone expect, miracles?"

I said, "I hope not."

Bodin threw me a curious look and said, "You heard about the note, I guess."

"On the radio."

He nodded and said, "I'll show it to you. It's in the safe."

Bodin disappeared through an inner door and returned a few minutes later with a manila envelope. He drew the note out and handed it to me. It read exactly as the announcer had stated, but the wording was done by pasting black strips of paper, cut in the form of letters, onto plain white paper. Bodin said, "Shrewd, hah?"

"Looks like somebody means business. Where was it postmarked from?"

"Right here. Paradise Village. The son of a bitch —excuse me, Robin—is right here among us."

Robin said, "What are you going to do about the ransom?"

Bodin shrugged his enormous shoulders and answered, "I don't know. What do you think, Mr. Callahan?"

"I think you should play along with this guy. Wait till the details for delivering the money are set, then weigh your alternatives."

Robin said, "Alternatives? Like what?"

"Whether to pay or set a trap. Meantime, get a rundown on anybody in town who might have experience with explosives from—let's say—military training and the like."

"I already thought of that. My men are digging into that, now."

37

I handed the note back to him and said, "I guess that's about it."

Robin looked from me to Bodin, then back to me again. She said, "You mean that's all you can do?"

"Yes."

Bodin shook my hand as I rose to leave, and asked if I was going to Doddard's funeral tomorrow. Robin said I was. Bodin said he'd see us there. I left his office feeling as though my life wasn't quite under my own control.

The sky was bright and a stiff wind churned up the sea as we walked back to the car. I said, "Chilly today."

"Mmm. Sure is."

"Bad day to be outdoors."

Robin cast a sidewise glance in my direction and said, "Any suggestions?"

"Let's go back to your place. I'm sure we'll accomplish wonders indoors."

I wasn't sure if it was the sense of adventure Robin felt at being included in a real-life murder case or a heightened feeling of admiration toward me for attempting to help Bodin, but, whatever, an almost uncontrollable passion seized her as soon as we returned to her home. The sun dropped out of the heavens and the moon popped up in its place without our ever having left the bedroom. Finally, I rolled over onto my back and said, "Whew! Better oil the bedsprings. They're smoking."

"Don't worry. The mattress is guaranteed for twenty-five years."

"Wish I could say the same for myself."

The sheet rolled off Robin's shoulders into her lap as she sat up. I was toying with the idea of wearing the guarantee out completely when Robin said, "How would you like some pork chops?"

Before my mouth could answer, my stomach growled. Robin laughed, bounced out of bed, and said, "I thought you would. Defrosted some this morning."

One appetite craved food, another craved something else. I closed my eyes until she left the room, then I hobbled into the bathroom and stood under an ice-cold shower until my desires stopped warring with each other.

Robin served the pork chops with macaroni salad and coleslaw. A bottle of beer washed it all down. I had a second bottle while Robin placed the dishes and utensils in the dishwasher. Finally, we retired into the living room. A third bottle of beer attached to my fist, I flopped down on the sofa and said, "You certainly know how to satisfy a man. How come you're not married?"

Robin, now clad in a terry-cloth mini-robe, curled up beside me, shrugged, and said, "Never found the right guy, I guess."

"You must have enough of them after you."

"In a way—yes."

"In a way?"

"Well, outside of tourist time, a town like this divides into two classes, the elite and the peasants, if you will."

"And you're a peasant?"

"No one's really a peasant, I guess. Or very few. But I'm certainly not one of the elite."

"What do you do for a living?"

"I'm a beautician."

"Really?"

"You sound surprised."

"Since you're so good at typing, I figured you for a secretary or something."

"I did typing in high school, but there's more money in hairstyling."

"You seem to do all right."

"After my father died, I inherited this house. All I pay is taxes, so the money stretches."

"What about your mother?"

"She died of cancer when I was little."

"What hours do you work?"

"It varies according to my boss's needs. Right now I'm on vacation."

"Why now? Better in the summer, no?"

"That's our busy season. Tourists and all. That's when I really make some tips."

"Uh-huh! I see. And how had you planned on spending your vacation before I dropped out of the sky?"

"Quietly. I'm trying to save to have my own business someday."

"A noble ambition. One worthy of the gods and other capitalists."

"Want another beer?"

"Love it, but I have a weight problem."

"Really?"

I glugged down the last remaining ounce before replying, "Sure. I finish one beer and can't *wait* for the next."

"You're hopeless."

Robin plucked the empty from my hand and disappeared into the kitchen. I flicked on the TV just in time to catch James Cagney's bullet-ridden figure staggering up the front steps of a church.

Robin returned with a refill and asked, "What's on?"

"Tail end of *The Roaring Twenties.*"

"Too bad it's ending. I love those old movies."

"I'm kind of addicted to stories of gangsters and murders myself, so long as I'm not starring in them."

In spite of the fact that my hand was stretched out like the paw of a begging dog, Robin hesitated with the bottle of beer. She said, "What's that supposed to mean?"

I thought of the passion that my being linked with the case seemed to arouse in her and said, "Nothing! Just—uh—thinking aloud about some of the cases I've—uh—been involved with in the past."

"Oh."

Robin nodded thoughtfully. She must have been relieved because she handed me the bottle. Sitting beside me, she said, "I'd really like to hear about your—oh—look!"

Robin pointed toward the TV. By some electronic miracle, Bodin managed to squeeze his figure onto her twenty-four-inch screen and still leave enough room for the faces of some onlookers and a microphone-filled hand. The same reporter who had questioned him previously about Doddard's murder asked, "What is your opinion concerning the blackmail note, Abner?"

Bodin's sudden stare made his blue eyes look like marbles. The reporter responded, "I mean, Sheriff—sir."

Bodin inhaled deeply, which must have caused the cameraman anguish, then spoke in slow, deliberate tones. "I don't rightly have an opinion.'

The reporter seemed surprised. "No opinion?"

"Well—uh—what I mean to say is—there could be many different reasons behind this note. Although I'm not certain, it could be just a prank by a sickie."

"A demented person, you mean?"

"I wouldn't think he was a quiz kid."

Bodin chuckled, his body shimmering like a mountain of jelly caught in an earthquake. When no one else joined the merriment, he snorted, coughed, and turned crimson. The reporter persisted, "Do you think it's possible the note is for real?"

"Anything's—um—possible in this world."

"If it—if it is for real—how do you intend to handle the situation?"

Bodin's shoulders went back and his chest puffed out as he confidently stated, "The best I can."

A dead silence fell over the TV. The onlookers glanced at one another while the sheriff stared blankly at the mike. Finally the reporter recovered his senses and asked, "Have you any leads at all?"

Bodin blinked his eyes like a man coming out of a trance, and said, "Leads? Of course I have leads and clues and things like that."

"Can you tell us the nature of these clues?"

Bodin folded his arms, closed his eyes, and sighed indignantly. He said, "Of course not."

The people around him shook their heads and muttered in disgust. Bodin's smug expression indicated a feeling of self-satisfaction as he faded from the screen.

The mayor's office was next to grace the picture tube. The little man looked rather impressive seated behind his massive oak desk. I wondered how many phone books he had underneath him. Paradise Village's seemingly solitary reporter pointed his microphone at the mayor and said, "Mr. Mayor, what's your opinion regarding the ransom—or tax note—in the Doddard case?"

Mayor Hanlon's solemn expression was highlighted by his large, cocker-spaniel-brown eyes. Folding his tiny hands in front of him, he said, "To be perfectly frank with you, I'm not certain. That is, quite possibly, a crank note. Though I shudder to think what sort of mind might find humor in such tragedy. Another possibility is that someone—not connected with the slaying—is trying to cash in on my good friend Sam Doddard's death."

The mayor's eyes lowered, his voice trailed off. The reporter prodded him. "Mr. Mayor, do you think the note could be for real?"

The mayor nodded gravely, his voice a mere whisper. "That's a distinct possibility."

"If it proves to be true, sir, might you conceivably authorize payment to prevent further murders?"

The cameraman must have been a real pro because the mayor actually seemed to grow as his hands clenched, then balled into fists. His sorrowful expression gradually tightened into a look of determination, which, I felt, had been carefully practiced before a mirror. His voice shook as he spoke.

"We are now living in an age of anarchy. Skyjackings, bombings, wanton murders daily fill our newspapers, radio, and television. To capitulate to anarchy is to deliver our very civilization into the

43

hands of barbarians, to leave our fate to the mercy of the savage. As long as I have breath in my body, this we shall never do."

The news ended on that note, followed by a ready-to-use douche commercial. Robin seemed enthralled. She said, "I think that's wonderful."

"I don't know. Plain water probably works just as well."

"Wha—? Oh! I'm talking about the mayor, stupid."

"I thought you didn't like him."

"I don't. But—there are times when he reaches you."

"He reaches me, all right. So does Bodin. Between them they took several minutes of viewing time without saying a goddamn thing."

"The mayor sounded very firm to me."

"Inflexible is the word. Sure sign of a damn fool."

"You think so? I—I kind of hoped he knew what he was doing."

I shrugged, wrapped my paw around her hand, and nodded toward the bedroom. "C'mon," I said. "I know what I'm doing."

Chapter Five

A fine, needle-like rain fell upon us as Father Moore read from Scripture to the largest non-underworld funeral gathering I had ever personally witnessed. Mrs. Doddard, veiled and clothed in black, mourned but did not weep. Facing us from the opposite side of the opened grave, her slim, squarely set shoulders and uptilted chin radiated an air of determination that was positively elegant. I nudged Robin and said, "There's a woman who can face life on its own terms."

An expression of uncertainty crossed Robin's face. She said nothing. The dignity of the event was marred somewhat by news photographers jockeying about for advantageous picture-taking positions. Sheriff Bodin, standing on the widow's left-hand side, was wearing a dark blue suit that must have fit him once. His complexion was plum-colored from his efforts to suck in his stomach before the cameras. His exertions were worthless, to say the least.

Flanking Mrs. Doddard on the right, eyes downcast, miniature hands folded, stood the mayor. Alongside him, trying unsuccessfully not to look bored, was his son. Burton's eyes kept roaming about the crowd, and more than once he had to stifle a yawn. When his eyes settled on me, he closed one hand into a fist.

I ignored him and turned my attention to the priest. He finished his prayers and sprinkled the casket, commending Doddard's soul to God. Wisely, he said no eulogy. Even the mayor had enough sense to keep his mouth shut. People filed up to the casket for a final prayer and to again extend sympathy to the widow. When our turn came, Mrs. Doddard shook hands with Robin and then with me. Beneath the veil, her large blue eyes were cool and steady. She said, "Thank you again, Mr. Callahan."

"I haven't done anything to be thanked for."

"Then accept my thanks in advance. I'm sure I'll owe them to you in the future."

Robin refused to take my arm as we walked back to the car. Although the lights dancing in her eyes looked green, I had the feeling that they should be red. She turned her head away as I reached to open the front door of my car for her. That very instant, a microphone was thrust at my face. A middle-aged man with mottled skin and iron-gray hair identified himself as a news reporter from a New York–based TV network. I didn't know him personally, though he looked familiar. Obviously, he knew me. He said, "Mr. Callahan, I'm Aaron Farmer. I covered your drug bust in New York—"

"Charmed, I'm sure."

"Sir, what is your opinion of Mr. Doddard's murder?"

"As I've said before, I have none."

"But you are professionally involved, correct?"

"Wrong. There goes your jackpot." Robin was glaring angrily at the drizzling sky. I held the door open and said, "Into the ark, please."

She didn't respond. The reporter brushed my lips with the mike and said, "Are you a friend of the Doddards?"

"No."

The mike shifted to Robin. "Are you a friend, ma'am?"

"Yes."

The mike swung back. "And you're a friend of hers?"

"Right now, that's debatable."

I left the door hanging open, walked around to the driver's side, and slid in behind the wheel. Farmer scooted away toward the mayor, who was helping Mrs. Doddard into her Rolls-Royce. I said to Robin, "Coming or staying?"

She placed her hands on her hips and said, "It would be just like you to leave me."

"It certainly would."

She hesitated, then climbed in beside me. I asked, "What the hell's bugging you?"

"Nothing. Nothing at all."

"Nothing is right. I can't even pay a small compliment to another woman without you going to pieces. You're jealous!"

"I am not!"

Robin glared at me as I coasted my Olds slowly behind the funeral procession and said, "You are, too! Not that I blame you, all things considered."

"Yes. You're a real prize."

By the time we hit town, Robin was mollified. All it took was thirty or forty assurances that my affections were solely hers. She was actually smiling as I braked to a halt in the Lighthouse parking lot. Robin looked at her watch and said, "All ready? It's only eleven thirty."

"Late to bed, early to rise, couple of beers, no more bloodshot eyes."

Adolph waved a soiled bar rag and favored us with a tarnished smile. He said, "Did the funeral go well, Mr. Callahan?"

"As well as funerals go, I guess. Two beers."

"One beer," Robin piped up. "I'll have ginger ale."

"Two beers," I said. "And give the lady a ginger ale. Speaking of funerals, aren't you working yourself into the grave? You're here day and night."

"When you own a business, you gotta watch it," Adolph said, serving our drinks. I hoisted the first foamy mug and swallowed everything but the glass. I said, "I'll sip the second one, Adolph. My stomach needs time to figure out what's happening."

"Ooh! Such a sense of humor. After a funeral, no less."

"And what a funeral," I said. "Television coverage and all."

Adolph looked surprised. "Even for the funeral?"

"Yep," I said.

"Do you think it's on now?"

"I can't think and drink at the same time. Better tune in your video marvel."

"He's back? That was popular in the fifties."

"That was Captain Video, Adolph. I'm referring to the enchanted box. Turn it on and watch the world revolve."

"You're so hysterical. I never know when you're serious."

Adolph flicked the channels around but came up with nothing but soap operas. I nursed several beers as the most tangled web of human tragedy, incest, rape, murder, and disease I had ever seen unfolded before my eyes. I might have missed a clue here and there, but, basically, I think the crux of the story was that the girl with the brain tumor who was raped by her fiancé who turned out to be her long-lost brother who was wanted by the police for armed robbery and murder ended up discovering in the final moment that she was really her mother's sister. Whatever, she died in time for a laxative commercial.

After all this, the beer seemed weak. I was ready to order a Scotch chaser when I was rescued by the news. The word *Bulletin* flashed across the screen. A harassed-looking announcer said, "Ladies and gentlemen, this morning this station, WPVR, received typewritten instructions concerning the so-called Death Toll demanded by Sam Doddard's killer. It read as follows:

" 'Fellow Citizens and Potential Victims:

" 'I order you to attend an emergency meeting tomorrow night, Wednesday, at Town Hall. Television coverage is essential. Before the cameras, one member of each household is to pay a toll of one hundred and twenty-five dollars a-piece for himself and each member of his immediate family. I use the male gender figuratively. Women are just as welcome in this enterprise. The money is to be paid in denominations of five-, ten-, and twenty-dollar bills. These bills are to be sealed in plastic sandwich foil before the TV

49

cameras, with the deliverer's signature written on plain paper and taped to the top bill inside the foil. I have a sample of the handwriting of every permanent resident of Paradise Village—a precaution I have taken to ensure that the money I receive is the citizen's and not a marked police substitute.

" 'I know that each permanent resident, except for one or two unsavory exceptions, has an account at the Paradise Village Bank. I have devised a plan to find out whether the bills are marked or not without endangering myself. Should they be, the bearer of whichever package I have drawn them from will die.

" 'These money packets are to be dropped into a burlap sack that will first be examined before the camera to ascertain its emptiness. Next, this sack will be entrusted to any able-bodied woman and child who will volunteer for the mission of delivering it to the appointed place. The volunteer will drive to All Hallow's Point at midnight. The child will carry or drag the sack up to the Hangman's Tree, drop it there, and return to the car. Woman and child will wait fifteen minutes, then drive back to town. No one is to leave their homes or Town Hall until the woman and child return. I swear no harm shall come to them.

" 'Remember, I walk among you. Any tricks, any failure to comply, will result in the death of someone's child. Cooperate and I shall disappear from your lives forever.

" 'P.S. Don't waste your time tracing this typewriter. It belongs to Miss Simmons, typing instructor in the Paradise Village High School. I am the perpetrator of that mysterious forced entry in which nothing was stolen.' "

Adolph said, "Dear me."

Robin said, "My God!"

I said, "Another beer, please."

As Adolph refilled my glass, the camera switched to the imposing figure of Sheriff Bodin. He was standing outside his office, mopping his forehead and jowls with a handkerchief. The reporter who was trying to interview him was having difficulty being heard because of the angry outcries and protests of the citizens surrounding Bodin. The sheriff said, "We—uh—can't be sure of—uh—the validity of this letter—"

Someone shouted, "You're never sure of anything but your paycheck, clown."

Another piped up, "Who's gonna protect our families when we're working?"

The reporter said, "Please—please—let the sheriff talk."

Bodin agreed. "Yes—uh—let me talk."

Everyone got silent. So did Bodin. Somebody yelled, "Say something! Say something, you dope!"

Bodin's balloon-like body swelled with indignation. He said, "Immediately upon being informed of this new development, I personally informed the mayor."

A heckler chided, "So what? If he has a radio, he'd know, anyway."

Bodin glowered and said, "Oh, yeah? Well, my report was official!"

The reporter said, "Sheriff, what was the mayor's reaction to the news?"

"Oh, he took it well."

"Did he say what action he wishes taken?"

"No, but he did say he was considering several solutions."

"What course of action do you favor at the moment?"

"I'd rather not reveal my plans, thank you."

Some of the spectators mumbled, others rolled their eyes. The reporter looked hopelessly disgusted. The picture faded back to the studio. The commentator said, "An aide to Mayor Hanlon has stated that the mayor will address the residents of Paradise Village tonight at seven from Town Hall in regard to this latest development. The mayor could not be reached for comment at the moment."

I said to Robin, "That's six hours from now. Let's go home and while away the time."

"Is that all you think about? With a madman running loose in town?"

"I assume he'll continue to run loose whether I'm vertical or horizontal. So—"

"So why don't you go over and help Sheriff Bodin?"

"He has enough company right now if you ask me."

"It seems your police expertise would be quite useful about now."

"Let me explain something about police expertise. We solve most of our cases by soliciting information from stool pigeons, rats, and finks. Bribes, threats, and promises are the tools we employ. I don't see how these tools could help me in this case because I don't know who, if anyone, to corrupt. At this point in time, my talents could be more useful in the barroom or the bedroom than in Bodin's office, *capisce?*"

"You're not even trying."

"That's because I'm not relaxed."

"Relaxed? What are you talking about?"

"I'm most deductive when my mind and body are relaxed. And you know what it takes to make my mind and body relax, don't you?"

Before she could answer, an odor, reminiscent of the Hudson River at low tide, entered the room. I asked, "Has Charley arrived?"

Robin looked over my shoulder and said, "He just floated in the door."

"That's not all that floated in the door."

The smell grew stronger as the footsteps drew closer. A friendly slap on my back was followed by the clever greeting, "Hiya, Sherlock!"

"Hello, Charley."

"Hi, ma'am."

"Hello."

"Whatta ya think of the latest development with this murderin' bum?"

"I haven't had time to think about it, Charley."

He winked, poked my chest gently with his elbow, and said, "C'mon! This is Charley you're talkin' to."

Robin's quite cool voice said, "Believe him, Charley. He hasn't given it a thought."

Charley scratched his stubble and said, "Really?"

"Yes, Charley. Robin's right."

Adolph appeared before all of us but focused his attention on Charley and said, "Would you like something to drink, or is this a social call?"

"I'll have a beer."

The public telephone rang and Adolph picked up the extension behind the bar as he handed Charley the beer. I heard him say, "What? Yes.

He's here. It's for you, Mr. Callahan. Sheriff Bodin."

As I took the receiver, Robin said, "See? I knew he'd need your help!"

I said, "Yes, Sheriff?"

"Mr. Callahan, the mayor's holding a press conference tonight—"

"I know. Saw the news."

"Would you—he wants you to come over to Town Hall. I could send a car for you."

"What? And tie up half your fleet?"

"Huh? Oh! Ha—ha. This is no time for jokes. This is serious business."

"What does he want with me?"

"He's—uh—calling on some of the town's leading citizens for advice. He has a plan to discuss with you."

My eyes were wandering over Robin's figure when I said, "I really don't think I can be of much help—" Robin kicked my left shinbone. "I'll be right over. I have my own car."

"Thanks. The mayor sure will appreciate this."

I handed the phone back to Adolph and said, "Mayor wants me. Got to go."

Robin said, "The mayor's office?"

"Yes. Coming?"

"No, thanks." She made a distasteful face. "I'll go home."

Adolph watched me with inquiring eyes, and Charley said, "What's up?"

"I winked, nudged his chest with my elbow, and said, "Official business."

I told Robin as much as I knew, dropped her off at home, and headed toward Town Hall.

The mayor's small body and large desk made him look like a pawn on an otherwise empty chess-board. He wasn't very impressive off camera. I leaned forward and swallowed his hand in mine. He said, "Good of you to come."

Standing beside the mayor was Bodin. The town's two clergymen occupied twin stuffed leather chairs by one wall. Everyone greeted me somberly. I greeted them back somberly and sat in one of two stuffed leather chairs by the opposite wall. The mayor said, "Mr. Callahan, I trust you've heard the conditions proposed to the residents of Paradise Village by this murderer? If he *is* the murderer."

"I have."

The mayor's eyes hardened, as much as cocker-spaniel eyes can harden, with righteous indignation. He thumped his desk with a childlike fist and said, "Surely you agree that we cannot endure such blackmail!"

All eyes were fixed on me. The clergymen nodded vigorously, in firm agreement. Bodin looked doubtful. I said, "Are you asking or telling me, Mr. Mayor?"

The mayor looked hurt. He said, "I'm asking, of course."

"No, sir. I do not agree with you."

The room got so quiet I began to feel drowsy. The mayor kept me awake by saying, "Surely you don't think we should accede to the demands of this fiend, do you?"

"What choice have you got?"

A frown darkened the Catholic priest's features as he said, "Mr. Callahan, we must always choose to fight evil, not surrender to it."

"No offense, Father, but will you have the courage to say those words to the mother of the next victim? He did say it would be a child, you know."

"I know. But if the proper precautions are taken—"

"Precautions? Have you a plan to watch all the children at all times?"

"Gen—gentlemen—may I interrupt?" It was the minister speaking. "H—how do we know the let—letter writer is the bom—bomber?"

"Sheriff!" I must have barked because Bodin nearly jumped out of uniform. "Did any of the typewriters in Miss Simmons's classroom match up with the typing on the note?"

"Yes. It was her very own machine."

"If I remember correctly, the school was broken into the very night before Sam Doddard died. Right?"

Bodin nodded nervously. "That's right. Mr. Callahan's right."

"Does that answer your question, Reverend?"

"It d—does."

"Mr. Callahan," the mayor said, "if we pay this blackmailer, he might demand more in the future, right?"

"It's a possibility."

"And when the news media spreads it all over the country, others might try it, too, correct?"

"Could be."

"Will you admit that our giving in to this monster could cause drastic repercussions throughout the country?"

"Anything's possible."

"Then we must not give in."

"If you mustn't," I shrugged, "you mustn't."

The mayor took a deep breath as though struggling to retain his patience. He said, "I'm aware of your reputation as a criminal expert, and thought you might render some useful advice, but it seems—"

I stood up, flaunted the palm of my hand to halt his banter, and said, "You didn't bring me here to give advice. You brought me here to endorse your conclusions. What's your plan? Vigilante patrols?"

The mayor looked distressed. He shuffled in his seat and said, "Armed-citizen patrols—"

"I thought so!" I indicated the clergymen with a sweep of my arm. "And these fine gentlemen are going to publicly endorse your scheme?"

"They happen to be of the same mind as me. Yes."

"I knew it! Why else would they be here? Who else could have more sway with the religious people than the clergy? Back their opinions of your plan up with the endorsement of a big-city cop and maybe even the atheists will buy the package."

"W—what would you suggest, Mr. C—Callahan?"

"Reverend, I'd pay the ransom. Hope the murders stop. Wait for the killer to make a slip. He obviously knows the town forwards and backwards. He must be a resident. If he sits on the money, it's no good to him. If someone starts spending bigger than usual, or leaves town, you'll have something to follow up."

The mayor said, "Just suppose he somehow or other gets away clean. What then?"

57

"So be it. At least we've saved some child from the cemetery."

Bodin said, "What if he ups the ante? Gets greedy?"

"Could be in our favor," I answered. "Success could lead to overconfidence, which, in turn, leads to mistakes."

The mayor slapped both hands on the desk in a gesture of finality. He said, "I will not yield to terror tactics. I will not face the people of this town and ask them to bow to the will of a murderer. I will not compromise with anarchy!"

"And I will not take up any more of your time," I said. "Hope we meet again, gentlemen. But not at somebody's funeral."

Robin was relaxing in a bikini when I returned to her house. A cool breeze filtered in through the opened windows and screen door. She said, "What's up?"

"Tell you for a beer."

"Deal."

I patted her rump as she glided past me into the kitchen. When she returned with the beer, I gave her a rundown on the afternoon's events. She said, "You really think the mayor's making a mistake?"

"Sure. This town could end up littered with bodies before the killer's caught."

"Don't say that." Robin shuddered.

"Speaking of bodies, how would yours like a whirl?"

"Don't you ever get tired?" Robin laughed. I'm bowlegged."

"Good!" I scooped her up in my arms, carried

58

her toward the bedroom, and said, "Someday I'll buy you a ten-gallon hat and point you west, but for now we'll just roll in the hay, pardner."

The alarm clock rang at 6:45 P.M. The thin sheet covering Robin's bare body rose and fell gently with her rhythmic breathing. I reached under the sheet, tickled her ribs, and said, "Rise and shine, or on thee I'll climb."

She pushed my hand away and said, "You really know how to knock a girl out."

"So long as it's *out* you're knocked, no sweat."

Robin chuckled as I sat up and flicked on the portable TV on the stand at the foot of the bed. "Think I'll make myself a drink before the mayor's speech comes on. I need some fortification to listen to that guy. Want something?"

"No, thanks."

I mixed a Scotch and soda and returned just as the somber-looking mayor appeared on the screen. He was seated behind his desk and was flanked by a clergyman on either side of him. A long-range shot revealed a host of town officials and leading citizens seated about the room. Mayor Hanlon said:

"Good evening, fellow citizens. As you undoubtedly know by now, a letter has been sent to Paradise Village's local TV station demanding a so-called Death Toll from our citizens in return for a promise to cease and desist from murdering us in the future. I will now read this letter for the benefit of anyone who may not as yet have learned of its contents."

The mayor slowly read the letter. By the time he finished, his face was grim and his voice emo-

59

tional. Finally, he said, "We cannot be certain this letter is genuine and not a hoax. However, although it does seem to be genuine, we can never, must never accede to the demands of those who would rule us by threats and terror.

"After much soul searching, I have decided that this anarchist must be resisted. Morality demands that we adhere to the time-tested principles of law and justice. The distinguished clergymen and civic leaders beside me tonight both aided and guided me in this decision. They concur unanimously with what I've just said.

"Now, I have outlined a plan to provide safety for all our citizens. It will require a joint effort on the part of local government, the police force, and, most importantly, you the citizen. The steps to be taken are as follows:

"One: Do not venture out alone or allow your children to play unsupervised. We want each block to form a watchdog committee to work in shifts so that at least one neighbor is alert at all times both day and night to oversee the block from his or her window. During the day, when the husbands go to business, we suggest the housewives congregate in each others' homes and pool their chores. While this will be inconvenient, at the moment it is vitally necessary.

"Two: We are asking for volunteers to supplement our police force by walking armed patrol through the neighborhood streets. Those of you who own guns may use them. We will provide and instruct those who don't. Please report to Town Hall tonight so that we may organize these patrols.

"While these measures may seem burdensome,

they are necessary and must be followed until the killer is apprehended. We will not, we cannot allow anarchists to threaten our own lives and the lives of those we love. We cannot, we must not, and we will not sacrifice ourselves and our children to the will of a mentally twisted murderer or a cruel, opportunistic prankster, whichever may be the case. We will begin organizing our citizen patrols immediately following this broadcast. Thank you and good night."

The cameras switched to the steps of Town Hall where Bodin and two of his deputies were trying to organize an already swelling crowd. Although wide-eyed with interest, Robin still had to stifle a yawn as she said, "What do you think of the mayor's plan?"

"I think it'll make the undertaker rich. Right now, everyone's in a fever. If this killer's smart, he'll either strike immediately to panic the people more, or lay low till they get careless, and then hit again. But these precautions won't stop him, I promise you."

"You're too pessimistic."

"Realistic's the word. What do you say we get dressed and venture about town? I'm anxious to watch the people's reaction to all this."

"Thank you, no." Robin yawned deeply. "I'm going back to sleep."

"Mind if I slip away for a bit?"

"Go ahead. I won't be much company to you, anyway."

Rolling my eyes lecherously over her sheeted figure, I asked, "Want anything before I go?"

Robin pulled the sheet up to her chin and burrowed her head beneath the pillow. "All right! All right!" I said. "I can take a hint."

I drove into the village and parked about a block away from Town Hall. People of all shapes, sizes, and ages milled about. The air crackled with excitement. Teenagers proudly brandished family rifles while older men grumbled indignantly about the gall of this anarchist daring to intimidate the town. The women were more restrained, though not necessarily subdued. Most seemed content to follow the leads of their mates, though more than one spoke of revenge and comeuppance. Even children clustered about, shooting each other with thumbs and forefingers.

The mayor had disappeared, leaving the job of organizing the mob to Bodin and his deputies. Overhead spotlights illuminated a long wooden table set up on the Town Hall lawn. An array of maps and time schedules lay on this table. Despite the fact that it was a clear, brisk evening, Bodin's cherry-like face oozed droplets of sweat as his newly formed army argued with him and each other over the timetables, areas to be covered, and order of command. Not wanting any part of this mess, I stayed deep enough in the crowd to keep out of the sheriff's sight. I listened to the excited laughter of the children and wondered what the killer was planning while the townsfolk were preparing against him. The probable answer to that question was enough to make the staunchest teetotaler want a drink.

Adolph and Charley were the only ones present when I entered the bar. I held my breath and joined them. Adolph said, "What would you like this time?"

"This time I'll have a Scotch and soda."

Charley said, "We was just watchin' the news before you came in. Some bunch of bullshit, huh?"

"Couldn't have said it better myself, Charley."

He agreed. " 'Course you couldn't."

Adolph's mouth hung open, showing the edges of his stained teeth. He shook his head, reached back and scratched the hump between his shoulder blades, and said, "Dear me. Do you think they'll catch this devil?"

Charley answered, "Sure! He'll screw up. You mark my words."

Adolph placed his hands on his hips, closed his eyes, and said, "I wasn't asking you, Charley." He turned to me and opened his eyes. "I was asking this gentleman."

Before I could comment, Charley interrupted, "It wouldn't hurt some folks to ask me a thing or two. There's lots I could tell if I so had a mind."

"That's the trouble with Charley, Mr. Callahan. He doesn't have a mind."

Adolph laughed merrily and I almost swallowed an ice cube. Charley said, "Might be a thing or two that could turn the tide on this laughin' match. Might be a thing or two old Charley could say that would turn these smiles upside down."

I said, "Like what, Charley?"

"He means the hump on my back," Adolph said. "But I've had it all my life, so I really don't mind a joke or two. I'm really very attached to it."

"Adolph!" I said. "I'm supposed to be the card around here, remember?"

"You know, Callahan, there's a thing or two I might mention about your little girlie that would make you feel like the joker in the deck."

"No, I don't know." I put my glass down and fixed my gaze on Charley. "But you better inform me. Fast!"

"I—now—don't be offended. I didn't mean no harm. Just don't like bein' laughed at, is all."

Adolph seemed to be busying himself cleaning glasses in order to avoid looking in our direction. I said, "Do you know something I should but don't, Charley?"

"Well—I mean, it's no disgrace or nothin'." Charley's beer glass began to shake in his hand. "Leastways not by today's standards."

"What's no disgrace, Charley?"

"Well—your friend, Robin, she was once—well—raped—"

"Raped!" Charley's face turned to stone. He froze in his seat. Adolph was wiping the bar so furiously I thought the rag would wear out. Calmly as I could, I asked, "Who raped her, Charley?"

"B—Burton Hanlon!"

"Hanlon!" Something must have happened to my face because Charley leaned backwards away from me and said, "Take it easy."

"When did this happen, Charley?"

" 'Bout five, six years ago. She was only a kid. It kinda broke her father up. He died not long afterwards."

"Details, Charley. I'm a cop, remember?"

"Yeah. Sure. It seems she was hangin' about with young Hanlon and the Pagan brothers—Hanlon's asshole buddies, ya know?"

"Have I ever seen these Pagan brothers?"

"Sure. They was the ones laughin' loudest at Hanlon's remarks the night you got dumped."

"Ah, yes. Go on."

"Well, seems they was all swimmin' or somethin', and it happened. Just them three and her. She reported it as rape. Boys sung a different tune. They was all under sixteen. Seems nothin' much was made out of it."

"Hanlon mayor at the time?"

"Sure was. Some say he had a hand in squashin' it all. But that's only hearsay—"

I heard the door open behind me and saw Charley's face sag. He swallowed hard, as though trying to suck back his spoken words. Looking around, I spotted Burton Hanlon and the Pagan brothers. They wore white dungaree jackets and pants and sported holstered pistols on their hips. They looked like three armed ice cream men. Hanlon snapped his fingers and said, "Three beers, Camelback. Make it snappy. We're on patrol."

Hanlon's attention turned to me. He said, "Well! If it isn't the wise-ass detective."

I turned my back to him without answering and faced my shaky companion. Hanlon shouted, "I'm talking to you, Callahan!"

I spoke to Charley in a voice loud enough to be heard by all. "C'mon. Let's get out of here."

Charley reluctantly followed me to the door, but Hanlon and his companions blocked our path. Hanlon smiled, slammed a closed fist into an open palm, and said, "Want to squeeze my hand now?"

I weighed the odds. The Pagan brothers were as big as Hanlon, and he was bigger than me.

65

Charley would be more hindrance than help, and they had guns. I chose the prudent course and said, "I don't want any trouble."

Hanlon pinched the discolored part of my cheek very hard and said, "Get the hell out of here and take your gutter buddy with you."

A full moon brightened the sky as we stepped into the cool night air. Anger made me tremble until I saw three bicycles, English racers, that were chained to the wood rail of the walkway that led back to the shore. An idea occurred to me that calmed my temper and made me chuckle. Charley shot me a look that he probably reserved for maniacs and said, "You find somethin' funny?"

I patted his back and said, "Charley, my boy, we're going to take a little ride."

I idled my car engine for five minutes while Charley fidgeted beside me. His nervous glance kept stealing toward the Lighthouse, and he continually asked, "What're ya waitin' for? Where we goin'? What're ya gonna do?"

I didn't bother to answer him. When three bicycle-riding figures emerged from the Lighthouse walkway, I said, "You'll have your answers soon, Charley. Very soon."

First I rolled my window down, then released the emergency brake and coasted out behind the peddling figures. Hanlon, the middle man, was slightly in the lead. I leaned heavily on my horn. Startled, the peddler on the right pulled closer to the curb while the other two veered to the left, near the middle of the road, which was just what I wanted. Passing the first rider, I pulled parallel to the leader, reached out and grabbed a handful of blond hair, and said, "Hi, punk!"

Hanlon gasped, nearly lost his balance, but managed to regain control of the bike. He shouted, "Let me go!"

"Make me."

"Are you nuts, or—"

Color drained from his face as I accelerated slightly. Behind me, the Pagan brothers were peddling like hell and shouting their lungs out. Next to me, Charley was jabbering incoherently. I said, "It's such a nice night, I thought we'd all take a ride together."

"You're crazy—"

"Know what it means in New York when someone goes for a ride, punk?" I pressed a little harder on the accelerator. "Do you?"

Hanlon's mouth hung open and he breathed in loud gasps. His knees shot up and down like pistons, and an oily sheen covered his chalky face. I laughed and said, "I'm going to kill you, Hanlon."

I pressed on the accelerator until his legs couldn't keep pace. His feet slid off the pedals. Wrists and hands were bloodless against the rubber steering grips. He closed his eyes, threw his head back, and screamed. It took me half a block to come to a full stop. By the time I did, every home in view was lit and people were running toward us.

When I released him, he fell off the bike and lay trembling on the ground. A crowd formed, with some of the men sporting guns. One of them trained a flashlight on Hanlon. I ignored their questions and pointed to a dark stain that was spreading across the front of his pants. I said, "That's your mayor's son, folks. Isn't he a pisser?"

Chapter Six

I awoke to the aroma of freshly brewed coffee. Robin's gay humming could be heard above the clatter of pots and pans. She had been sleeping when I returned last night, so I didn't have a chance to tell her what had happened. I pulled on my trousers and tiptoed into the kitchen. Robin was working by the stove in a rose-colored bikini. Sneaking up behind her, I threw my arms around her naked belly and kissed her savagely on the neck. She followed a sharp intake of breath with this remark, "Whew! The eggs can wait."

I smacked her behind and said, "No! The eggs can't wait. I worked up a terrific appetite last night."

"Oh?" She threw me a puzzled glance. "How?"

"I did a little job on the mayor's punk."

Robin slid the spatula under two fried eggs, lifted them, and froze. Her eyes narrowed. "What did you do?"

"Turn the eggs," I urged. "Turn the eggs."

"What? Oh—yes."

Robin flipped the eggs without breaking the yolks. I gave her a detailed rundown of my clash with the mayor's son while we ate. Her facial expressions ran from anger to delight. Then she frowned and said, "What if he presses charges?"

"Don't worry. The publicity would be humiliating for the mayor. Especially when I went into detail about how the chip-off-the-old-block peed his pants."

"But don't you see? They might never hear your side of the story."

"Are you kidding? This is America. We have a free press."

"Paradise Village's only free press is run by one of our millionaire mayor's closest millionaire friends, Rollo Pagan."

I missed my mouth with a forkful of egg. "Did you say Pagan?"

"Yes."

"He has two sons?"

"Yes."

"Bad news."

"They were present?"

"And how."

"Bad news is right."

Just then a knock came to the door. Robin volunteered to answer it. A few seconds later she called my name. Bodin's frame blocked the doorway. His thumbs were hooked in his gunbelt, and his fingers toyed nervously with the buckle. He said, "I—uh—Mr. Callahan—"

"Are you placing me under arrest?"

"Uh—yes, sir—with your permission—I mean—"

"And what, pray tell, are the charges?"

"Assault—uh—"

"You mean my little session with young Hanlon?"

69

"Yes, sir. We—I mean, the mayor said—I hate to tell you this, but—he said either you leave town and never come back or he'll press charges against you for assaulting his son, reckless driving, and whatever else he can think of."

I finished dressing, pressed my wrists together, and held them straight out. "Cuff me, Officer. Do your duty."

"Aw—look—why make this tough?"

"I insist. Robin, have you a camera?"

"Yes. A Polaroid."

Bodin glanced nervously toward her as I said, "Then you must take a picture of me manacled. I wouldn't let my big-shot reporter friends miss this for the world."

Bodin, who had taken the cuffs from his pouch at my insistence, dropped them on the floor. He said, "Big-shot reporter friends?"

"Not to mention police and politicians. When you spend twenty years as one of New York's Finest, you make friends as well as enemies."

Bodin stared at the cuffs on the floor and said, "Oh, my!"

"I'll get them." Robin picked up the cuffs and handed them to Bodin. "Why ruin a good pair of pants?"

"Really!" Bodin shook his head. "That wasn't very nice."

Robin disappeared into the bedroom while I forced Bodin to handcuff me. She returned with the Polaroid, aimed it, and said, "Look oppressed."

I dropped my manacled hands. The cuffs struck my groin. My pained expression was for real. Robin said, "Excellent! That's great!"

"You don't know how much I'm putting into it."

Bodin looked ill at ease. He shuffled his feet and said, "Can we go now?"

"Don't be in a hurry," I told him. "I've got to make sure my picture came out."

"It did," Robin said. "It's beautiful."

I checked it over, agreed with her, and said, "Can we use the siren, Sheriff? I want this to look official."

Robin stashed the picture and said she'd follow in my car. Up till now, I hadn't known she could drive. I threw her the keys and said, "After you, Sheriff."

Bodin refused to use the siren, so we rode in silence until a message crackled across the two-way radio.

"Sheriff Bodin. Calling Sheriff Bodin. Do you read me?"

Bodin clicked the return button and said, "I read you, Dick. What's up?"

"Trouble at Mrs. Doddard's house."

"Oh, Christ! What's happened?"

"Don't rightly know. Better haul ass over there. Servants said something about her screaming and a picture—couldn't get the story straight."

Bodin glanced at me, then asked, "Did you dispatch another car?"

"How could I? We only got two beside yours. One's laid up with muffler trouble, and the other one doesn't answer. They're probably having coffee."

"Ah! For Christ's sake—"

"Don't blame me, Abner. It's not my fault."

"O.K.! O.K.! Soon's you hear from them, send 'em over to meet me."

"Sure."

The sheriff's eyes and chest swelled as he barked, "Yes, *sir!*"

"Yes—yes, sir!"

"And call me sheriff durin' working hours."

"Yes, sir, Sheriff."

"And remember you don't tell your superiors to haul ass."

"Yes, sir, Sheriff. No haulin' ass."

A satisfied smirk crossed Bodin's lips as he shot me another look. Then his mind must have started working again because the smirk changed to a frown and he said, "I wonder what's goin' on now?"

The lean, distinguished butler who had greeted us with so sophisticated an air during the wake was now disheveled, pasty-faced, and in a state of considerable nervous agitation. He didn't even notice my handcuffs as he said, "Thank God you're here, gentlemen. Thank God! This way. This way."

We ran behind the servant into the house and followed him up a curved staircase into Mrs. Doddard's bedroom. A maid sat on the bed cradling her mistress's head in her lap. She spoke soothingly and fed the prostrate woman drops of water. Mrs. Doddard's glazed eyes focused on us. She said, "Oh, God! They murdered him! My God!"

She began to tremble and cry. The maid said, "Why don't ye be gettin' the doctor instead of standin' there gapin'?"

Bodin said, "Didn't you call him?"

"Of course! Do you think we're bloomin' eejits?"

Bodin scratched his head and said, "Why, no. Of course not. But if you already called him—"

"Aren't ye the police? Light a fire under him!"

This lofty conversation was interrupted when Mrs. Doddard said, "The picture! Find the picture! It's on the floor someplace."

"Picture?" Bodin said. "What picture?"

"It came in the mail—dropped it when I got dizzy—"

Falling on handcuffs and knees, I spotted an envelope under the bed. It was postmarked Paradise Village and addressed to Mrs. Doddard. Fishing about a little more, I came up with a Polaroid picture that made me nauseous. I stood up and handed it to Bodin. He caught his breath, then said, "Holy Good Christ!"

At that moment, a short, plump man entered the room, carrying a black leather bag. He glanced at my cuffs and looked quizzically at the sheriff. Bodin said, "It's all right, Dr. Barnes. Mr. Callahan's all right."

"Get the hell out of here!" the good doctor snapped. "Both of you!"

"Yes, sir!" Bodin said, waddling away as fast as his massive thighs would allow. I followed suit. When we reached the car, I said, "Will you take these frigging cuffs off me?"

He said, "I don't know. You did ask for them."

"Do you want my help or don't you?"

"Don't get excited, Mr. Callahan. I wasn't very serious."

I looked about for Robin but didn't see her. I

figured we must have lost her when we changed course. Bodin fumbled with the keys and finally set me free. I said, "Let's get to the church. Fast."

We arrived within minutes and found the door to the rectory unlocked. Bodin was familiar with the place and led me right to the priest's study. After a slight hesitation, he opened the door. Father Moore's long, lean body lay crucified on the floor. He was spreadeagled, and nails had been driven through his hands and feet. Barbed wire formed a bloody crown about his head. The gaping wound in his side was probably what had finished him. Written in blood on the floor beside his body were the words: HE DIED FOR YOUR SINS.

A Polaroid camera similar to Robin's lay on his desk. Bodin staggered out of the room and I followed behind him. He leaned against the stair rail, breathing heavily. I patted his shoulder and said, "You O.K.?"

"Yeah. Yeah."

"Who the hell was watching this block last night?"

"He—the priest was—during the early part of the night. Eight to midnight, I believe."

"That makes sense. He'd been in on the plan before the mayor announced it. So he'd naturally be one of the first to volunteer."

"Yes. He was. Right after you left yesterday, he did."

"What time is your last mail pickup at night?"

"I think—eleven."

"Then he was probably killed during his watch by somebody he knew. Somebody who had the mail pickup figured so the picture would arrive at Mrs. Doddard's residence this morning."

"Yeah! The connivin' bastard! Made us think he was after a kid and then kills a grown-up. Tried to distract us, that's what."

"I hate to sound like I'm sticking up for him, but he didn't exactly lie."

"He didn't lie!" A look of anger crossed Bodin's face, and for the first time since I'd known him, I felt a bit wary. "What the hell do you mean, he didn't lie?"

"Sheriff—everybody—no matter what their age —is somebody's child."

Chapter Seven

Sam Doddard's murder had received only moderate coverage from the press, whereas Father Moore's hit the other extreme. Reporters descended upon Paradise Village like boll weevils on a cotton crop. The governor, who was suffering from ill health and was reputed to have favored Mayor Hanlon to be his successor in the next election, offered the assistance of the state police with the advice—according to Bodin—that failure to solve this problem could terminate the mayor's political career.

During the next few days—upon seeing no progress from the police and hearing nothing from the killer—the citizens of Paradise Village began to show the effects caused by mounting tension. There were two cases of women being rushed to the hospital for taking overdoses of barbiturates. One lived; one died. A man named Guy Sorrel, who owned a charter fishing boat and had lived in Paradise Village for twenty-five years without ever having been known to take a drink, got drunk, killed himself and severely injured another driver in an automobile accident. Except for police and civilian patrols, the streets were deserted at night. Neighbors grew cool toward each other. Strangers were totally shunned. I began to imagine how the average decent German or Russian citizen felt under the reign of Hitler or Stalin.

Father Moore's murder seemed to have eliminated whatever charges the mayor and the police had against me. After leaving the rectory, I found Robin in the sheriff's office. She had driven there by an alternate route and become puzzled when we failed to show up. Naturally, my explanation shocked her. The town officials were also shocked. So much so, I guess, they just forgot about my offense.

Robin and I attended the priest's funeral along with most of the town's inhabitants. A young, heavy-set priest with a Rasputin-like black beard had been commissioned to take over the parish. He performed the funeral services. Though the same people attended as had at Doddard's funeral, they were far more subdued. Mrs. Doddard, in spite of the emotional strain she was suffering, also attended. She wore black and wept freely. Afterwards, ignoring questions from the press, the people rushed back to their homes. As we entered the car, I said, "Feel like taking a walk by the shore, Robin?"

"If you want."

"Good. I have some thinking to do."

Fifteen minutes later, I parked by the shore and we strolled hand in hand through the sand. The breeze was just vigorous enough to counter the sun's strong rays and keep us comfortable. My thoughts got the best of me and I kept silent until Robin said, "Have you forgotten I'm here, or is your tongue on strike?"

"My tongue is working, as you well know."

"Then use it."

"Here? Suppose someone catches me?"

"To talk with, dummy. I'm in suspense."

"So am I. Why in hell would this guy mail the priest's picture to Mrs. Doddard?"

"So! She's the one you're thinking about."

"In a professional capacity only. Now, answer me. Why?"

"Who knows? The police seem to think it was to cause a great sensation."

"Possible. Though the murder itself was sensational enough. Now, according to the news media, the sheriff's office and the state police have also brilliantly concluded that Father Moore must have known the killer since he was on watch and there was no sign of forced entry, correct?"

"Yes. Sounds reasonable."

"It's also reasonable that a priest would admit anyone, even a stranger, if he thought their visit was an emergency call, right?"

"I suppose."

"Just a thought. Although the priest must have known everybody in town, at least by sight, so the police theory is probably true."

"Have you formed any definite theory of your own?"

"Sort of. I think there's more to this harassment of Mrs. Doddard than meets the bloodshot eyeball."

"Oh?" Robin's tone cooled and she looked definitely annoyed. "Just what do you think is behind it?"

Robin's candid jealousy amused me. I said, "I really can't tell until I have a frank, private discussion with the lady."

Robin said not another word but stared quietly out at the ocean for the remainder of our walk. She had cooled off by the time we returned to her house and proved her affection by mixing my first Scotch and soda of the day. I sat back on the sofa, propped my feet up on the coffee table, and sipped contentedly while watching the afternoon movie on her TV. *The Maltese Falcon* was showing, and I got involved. Robin was puttering around the kitchen and Humphrey Bogart was slapping Peter Lorre when a news bulletin interrupted the story. A grim-faced commentator said, "Ladies and gentlemen, a new threat has been issued by the alleged murderer of Sam Doddard and Father Moore. A copy was received in the mail today by this station and also by the mayor's and sheriff's offices. The words were clipped from newspaper print and pasted to plain white paper to form sentences. The postmark was Paradise Village. It reads as follows:

" 'Dear Potential Victims:

" 'You have evaded paying your Death Toll. Uncle Sam fines you when you cheat on taxes. So shall I. Your bill has just increased one hundred percent. I now demand two hundred fifty dollars tax for each Paradise Village citizen. Tomorrow evening you are to call a meeting for collection and delivery of one-half million dollars, following the same rules that were originally issued to you.

If these terms are not complied with, another soul will wing away from our fair village and a steeper fine will be imposed.

"'Very sincerely,
"'The Toll Collector.'"

The commentator ended the quote and said, "We have not been able to reach either the mayor or the sheriff for comment. Any further developments will be reported immediately."

I looked up and saw Robin standing beside me rigid and frightened. She said, "Oh, my God!"

"Amen! They better pay this guy, or he's going to solve the population explosion."

"Do you think they will?"

"Who the hell knows? I need another drink. Want one?"

"Just Coke."

While in the kitchen, I heard a car pull into the driveway. A few seconds later there was a sturdy knock at the door. When I returned to the living room, I met Bodin, who was again wearing that ill-fitting blue suit. Agitation marked his features. I said, "Greetings, Sheriff. Like a drink?"

"No—yes. Beer."

Robin volunteered to get it. I said, "Sit down. Didn't see you at the funeral."

"I didn't go. The people are after my ass. I'm even afraid to be seen. That's why I'm not in uniform."

I hardly considered his suit proper camouflage. I said, "Pressure's on, eh?"

"Been gettin' threatenin' phone calls. Someone threw a rock through the office window last night. They're blamin' me for these murders—this—this trouble. You'd think it was my fault or somethin'."

"Fear brings out the worst in all of us. What can I do for you?"

Robin returned with the beer. Bodin swallowed two-thirds of the twelve-ounce bottle with one gulp. He said, "I need your help. I'm catchin' the shaft in this deal. The mayor has more confidence in the state police than he has in me, so they're runnin' the show."

"So? Doesn't that take the heat off you?"

"Unofficially, yes. Officially, they're lendin' assistance and I'm in charge. If we nail this guy, the mayor will appease the governor by givin' the state police most of the credit. If we don't catch him, the mayor will keep the governor happy by lettin' the blame drop on me. Either way, I get screwed."

"How can I help? What can I do?"

"I—I don't know, myself. I just figured with your experience you might have some ideas or somethin'."

"I've already told you what my idea was. The mayor wasn't very receptive to it. And after that incident with his son, I don't think he'll warm up to me very much now."

Bodin waved a fat hand and said, "Forget about that. It's the last thing on his mind right now. If you could help solve this problem, he'd give you the key to the village. Besides, his son's been in trouble before."

I looked at Robin and said, "So I've heard."

Her face flushed the color of her hair. She looked away from me, sipped her Coke, and said, "Let me get you another beer, Sheriff."

"Thanks."

I said, "Have you seen the mayor today?"

81

"Yes. He's in his home with a captain from the state police. A group of villagers demonstrated outside it earlier today. His servants have standard orders to say he's out of town seeking expert help from top criminologists on the problem."

"I bet that set well with the local citizenry."

"They were pissed off."

"What's he doing with the captain?"

"Trying to figure out a new strategy. I asked the mayor if it was all right for me to come to you for advice and he said he didn't give a damn what I did. Seems the captain heard of you. Told me to come fetch you—if you want to come, that is."

Robin returned with his beer and eyed me steadily. I shrugged. "Why not? How do we get there without encountering demonstrators?"

"They were gone when I left. Otherwise I wouldn't've left."

"You're thinking, Sheriff. You certainly are."

The mayor lived in a modest mansion surrounded by a lot of acreage. He obviously sank more of his money into the earth than on top of it. His tiny hand disappeared into mine as we met in his living room. He said, "Good of you to come, Mr. Callahan."

"Nice of you to invite me."

He cast an odd look in my direction, then introduced me to a giant of a man in a brown uniform. "Mr. Callahan, meet Captain Edison."

A strong white smile flashed across Captain Edison's large, bony face as he buckled my knees with a handshake. "Pleasure to have you along, Mr. Callahan. I remember your dope bust in New York. How's the punctured lung holding out?"

"Sound as a Cuban peso."

The mayor grunted and said, "Are you still as adamant about our paying off the perpetrator as you originally were?"

"More than ever. You've seen the results you've obtained by holding out."

Edison said, "What can we expect if we pay off, Mr. Callahan?"

"We can expect the murders to cease."

"And how do we bring the perpetrator to justice?"

"I don't know. We can hope he slips up with the money somehow. We can watch out for any resident who changes his life-style or moves away."

"Or we can pay out the money and never catch the criminal, right?"

"That's a possibility, Captain."

"Hardly a satisfying one."

"I find it more satisfying than having another murder on our hands."

"I think we can prevent another murder and catch our killer."

"How?"

"At the risk of sounding immodest, let me say that I'm the finest sharpshooter on the state police force today."

"So?"

"I've studied the area in which the money is to be dropped. I've also found a tree on top of a grassy knoll about a quarter of a mile from the spot. From this vantage point, using a high-powered rifle with an infra-red scope, I feel positive I can pick this killer off when he attempts to take the suitcase."

"Suppose you're wrong?"

"If I miss, he'll probably get away with the money, in which case we shouldn't have any more trouble from him."

"Suppose he panics and runs without the money?"

"Well—then—"

"Well—then—we'll have to worry about one angry murderer, won't we?"

"Odds are he'll still get caught. I could have other men planted in the area."

"That's risky. This guy seems to know everything that goes on in and around this village. I doubt you could sneak a team of men anywhere within miles of here without his knowledge."

"You're right. The extra men was just an afterthought. Originally, I intended to go it alone. I guess that's best."

"Mr. Mayor," I said, "if you advise the town citizens to pay up, then you blow your scheme, how do you think they'll react?"

"I'll not advise them of anything. I'm announcing an emergency meeting at the Town Hall this evening where I am going to put the question of payment squarely on the shoulders of the voters."

"If they vote to pay, what then?"

"I'll put the captain's plan into effect."

"You must have a lot of confidence in him."

"He has assured me he will not fire unless he is absolutely sure of hitting his mark."

Edison said, "The mayor has nothing to fear. If I have the slightest doubt in my mind about my ability to cut him down with one shot, I won't fire."

"You'll let him loose with the money?"

"Absolutely."

"What if he has confederates? Suppose you kill him, and somebody else continues his grisly work?"

"The mayor, Sheriff Bodin, and I all think it's the work of one or possibly two men. After all, you don't employ an army for an operation like this. The more people involved, the more likely somebody will crack and spill the beans."

"I'll buy that. But what if he spots you? Just think of the consequences."

"I was a commando in Korea. I know how to keep from being spotted."

"Just for argument's sake"—I turned to the mayor—"suppose he does get spotted or the killer doesn't show. Suppose he kills again and blames you for setting a trap. How will that set with the citizens?"

"I'll simply deny everything." The mayor shrugged. "It will be my word against the murderer's."

I shook hands with Edison and the mayor before leaving. It was, at best, a halfhearted formality for all concerned. Nobody offered their hands to Bodin, so I shook his, which was, I suppose, a silly gesture since he was driving me back to Robin's place. He seemed pretty disgusted when he dropped me off. Robin greeted me with a kiss and said, "How'd everything go?"

"Waste of time. I'll fill you in while you make me a Scotch and soda."

"O.K."

I briefly outlined their plan. Robin said, "You could tip the people off, you know."

"Nope. I was brought in as a confidant. Besides, if I blow the whistle, who knows how the killer will react. He might just kill someone else and then the people might idolize the mayor and Captain Edison while blaming everything on me."

"So—what will you do—nothing?"

"That was my intention when I came to this—this—so-called Paradise."

Robin lowered her eyes and said, "When the chips are down, you're just like everybody else."

I planted my drink on the coffee table with a thud and said, "Now what the hell is that supposed to mean?"

Robin's complexion darkened. She said, "How much do you know about—about my trouble with Burton Hanlon?"

"I—uh—I understand he raped you."

"Who told you?"

"Charley."

"Figures. Though I suppose you would have found out eventually, anyway."

"Look. You don't have to discuss it. I mean—it's not really my business."

"I want you to know." Robin pressed my hand with both of hers. "I feel very special about you. If I didn't—we wouldn't have—what I mean is—"

"I know, baby. You don't have to spell it out. I feel the same way about you."

"You don't have to say that."

"It's true."

"I—I hope so—but whatever—I've slept with you because I'm in—well—infatuated with you."

"I'm glad. I'm really happy to know this."

"I'm not just an easy lay. I never was. I'm not

innocent, but I don't flop with every guy that makes a pass at me, either."

"You didn't have to tell me. After twenty years on the force, I can spot that kind."

"I should have realized." Robin's eyes bored into mine. "There must be lots of things that you can see that others can't. I said I was no innocent and I'm not. Thanks to the mayor's son. Six years ago—I was only fifteen at the time—I had been swimming near my home when Burton Hanlon and the Pagan brothers came biking by. They saw I was alone. It was kind of early in the morning and a bit cool to be bathing, but I loved the water, so it didn't really matter to me. Anyhow, they walked down by the shore and waved to me. I was flattered—I mean, the mayor's son and all. He had never noticed me in school or anything. I came out of the water and dried myself off and —well—flirted a bit. You know what I mean?"

"Uh-huh."

"Well, the Pagans shied off and Burton and I took a stroll through the sand dunes. We joked and fooled around a little. There wasn't much to the bathing suit I was wearing and he got itchy fingers. At first it was tickling—a little feel here and there—a kiss—I didn't object too strenuously until he became rambunctious. Then I told him to stop. He grew angry. Said I was a tease. Then he grabbed me. We struggled. I screamed, but he covered my mouth, then shoved sand into it. I gagged and choked while he—he raped me."

Robin became visibly shaken. Her complexion paled. I poured some Scotch and made her drink it straight. Pink flecks began to color her cheeks. I said, "Were you a virgin when this happened?"

She nodded and said, "My screams brought the Pagan brothers. It didn't take Burton long to finish with me. He was buttoning his pants when they arrived. He invited them to participate, and—well—they did. More than once. Finally, they warned me to keep my mouth shut and left."

"What happened then?"

"I just lay there. I don't know for how long. At last, I put my suit on and went home. I stayed in my room crying until my father came home and found me."

"What did you tell him?"

"The truth. He was so shocked he could hardly talk. Finally, he called Sheriff Bodin."

"Bodin was sheriff at the time?"

"Yes. That was his first term. He sympathized with me until he heard me accuse the mayor's son. That panicked him. Still, he went about his duty and took me to the hospital and all. But he was upset about the whole affair. While I was being treated, he left my father in the hands of his deputies and went to see the mayor. Later on, he explained rather meekly that the mayor sent his regrets and offered to pay any sum within reason as compensation."

"I can imagine your father's reaction."

"He stormed about, swearing and making threats. But he wasn't a violent man, and after a few minutes, he broke down and cried. Bodin advised me not to worry, and drove Dad home. The following morning my father died in a crash while driving to pick me up."

"Where did the accident take place?"

"Near the hospital. The road leading up to it is on a hill that gives a beautiful bird's-eye view of the shoreline. But it has some sharp turns. He took one too fast, lost control, and was killed. As far as I'm concerned, he died because his concentration was off. I can thank the mayor and his son for that."

"What happened with the rape charge?"

"Sheriff Bodin convinced me to drop it."

"Oh?"

"He explained what a rape trial is like—the cross-examination you go through and everything. He told me the boys' story was that I offered my body for money and cried rape when they wouldn't pay. It was their word against mine, he said, and I didn't have much of a chance. But I was so outraged, I didn't care. I wanted to fight them, anyway."

"Why didn't you try?"

"Sheriff Bodin explained that the Hanlons and the Pagans influenced practically every business in the village. No juror who valued his livelihood would convict those boys. All I would accomplish would be the smearing of my own reputation. After thinking it all out, I realized he was right."

"What happened after you dropped the charges?"

"Everything was hushed up nicely. The rumors faded and the townspeople acted as though nothing had ever happened."

"You remained here alone?"

"Yes."

"Even though a minor?"

"The law in this town wanted me quiet. They weren't about to belabor so small a point."

"Didn't you have anyone to turn to? Anyplace else to go?"

"I have no relatives and this has always been my home. I wasn't about to move anywhere. Besides, Sheriff Bodin used to visit me fairly regularly, just to see that I got along O.K."

"How did you support yourself?"

"My father's insurance kept me going until I was old enough to work. One of his colleagues acted as my legal guardian to administer the annuity, but otherwise I was on my own."

"What kind of work did your father do?"

"He was an executive at the Paradise Savings Bank. We were never rich, but he made a decent living."

"Did the mayor come across with any cash?"

"Nope. Once he knew he was safe, it slipped his mind."

"I guess Bodin was happy when you dropped the charges."

"Yes, poor man." Robin smiled sadly. "The only reason he was elected sheriff was because of Mayor Hanlon's support. I can imagine what might have happened to his little career if he hadn't got me off the mayor's back."

"It's not hard to imagine," I said, taking her into my arms, "not hard at all."

Robin and I spent the rest of the afternoon watching TV and making love. During one of our rest periods, a news bulletin announced the mayor's emergency session at Town Hall. It stated the reasons for the session and invited all citizens to attend. Phones were to be installed so that those people who could not attend might call in their opinions. I was pretty certain what the outcome would be. Robin phoned in her opinion

90

and by 11:00 P.M. my own was confirmed. A special televised public meeting was set up for the following morning. The people had voted 100 percent in favor of paying the Death Toll.

Chapter Eight

I woke up the next morning with a definite task in mind. During breakfast, I said, "Robin, last night I dreamed someone had thrown loose pieces of a puzzle against a large ceiling fan. The blades scattered them across the room. Some pieces fell into their proper places. Others didn't. I'm going to work on those others today."

Robin clapped her hands and said, "You're onto something?"

"Possibly."

"What?"

"I'd rather not say just yet."

"Why not?"

"Because it's merely a hunch that could lead nowhere."

"Tell me, anyway."

"Nope." I pecked her lips. "Gotta go."

"Can I come with you?"

"No. But I shall return."

A wary gleam entered her eyes and she spoke in a tone that might have chilled an Eskimo. "Are you going to see *her?*"

I gripped her shoulders, spun her around, and smacked her behind. I slipped through the door and, while closing it, said, "Curious little devil, aren't you?"

I drove by the town square to observe the turn-out. Masses of people formed lines entering or exiting the village bank and Town Hall. Cameramen and news reporters filmed and questioned the inhabitants. It took me twenty minutes to drive one-quarter of a mile. Finally, I turned down a side street, found a less-congested road, and headed for Mrs. Doddard's residence.

A smile of recognition flickered about the butler's mouth when he answered my knock. "Good morning, Mr. Callahan. I'm afraid Mrs. Doddard isn't home at the moment."

"I should have called before coming. Expect her home soon?"

"Most probably. Come in, sir." I followed him into a spacious, airy room. Louvered doors opened onto a curved marble balcony that commanded an aerial view of the town. He seated me at a rounded glass patio table shaded by a large umbrella. He coughed delicately, lowered his voice, and said, "Mrs. Doddard has gone to pay her share of the toll, sir."

"Don't you double as chauffeur?"

"Only when she uses the Rolls. Today she took the Mercedes."

"Oh."

"She insisted on delivering the money personally so this lunatic would have no doubts about her contribution."

"She's quite a woman."

"Yes, sir. That she is. May I offer you some refreshment?"

93

"Coffee would be fine. Cream, no sugar."

"Very good, sir."

The butler returned with a silver pot of coffee and a thick china mug. He poured me a cup and excused himself. I enjoyed the breeze, the view, and the coffee. Just as I drained my cup, Mrs. Doddard showed up. She made a plain black dress look quite appealing. She said, "Mr. Callahan, how nice to see you."

I took her hand and replied, "The pleasure's mine. Believe me."

I held a chair for her, then resumed my own seat. Mrs. Doddard said, "More coffee?"

"No, thanks."

The butler materialized magically and cleared the table. When he disappeared, Mrs. Doddard said, "I assume your visit is in connection with this—this—uh—"

"Yes. There are one or two aspects about this case that have aroused my curiosity. Maybe you can enlighten me on a few points."

"I'll be glad to try."

"The general opinion fostered by the killer and accepted by the community is that your husband was chosen as a victim at random to stress the point that this killer was not bluffing. Do you accept this?"

"I—I really don't know what else to think."

"Can you think of any reason the killer would want to send that horrible picture of Father Moore to you?"

"I—I'm not sure." She bit her lower lip and frowned. "The sheriff thinks it was sent to further torture me, which would, in turn, horrify the villagers. It would stress the total ruthlessness of this man."

"That point doesn't sit well with me. What could better stress his ruthlessness than the very murders themselves? Now that you've told me what the sheriff thinks, tell me what you think."

"I'm not sure what to think."

"Were you and Father Moore personal friends?"

"Yes. But most people in town could say the same thing."

"May I speak frankly?"

"Of course."

"Were you and Father Moore lovers?"

"Oh, Mr. Callahan!" Mrs. Doddard placed one hand against her forehead and laughed heartily. Finally, she wiped her eyes and said, "If ever a male virgin over the age of sixteen existed, it was John Moore."

"How do you know?"

"We dated at the state university. It's the college closest to Paradise Village."

"Oh?"

"Even then he was a born priest. Religion was always uppermost in his mind."

"Always?"

"Always. And that was the era of parking and petting if you remember."

"I remember."

"Whenever we parked, I did all the petting. If it weren't for my lukewarm advances, we might have been brother and sister. Except for the fact that I had so many other callers, I would have doubted my femininity."

"You can rest easy about that. You say you had a lot of callers, eh?"

"Quite a few."

"Well, since it's easy to see that you're a person of selective taste, you must have rejected quite a few suitors."

"Yes. Quite a few. John was the only one who rejected me. The church was his first love."

"When did you meet Mr. Doddard?"

"Shortly after I gave up on John. Abner Bodin had to quit college to support his family, so he went to work in what is now Doddard's Body and Fender Shop. At the time it belonged to an elderly gentleman named Turin. Anyhow, I stopped by one afternoon while he was working to cancel a date we had. Something had come up, though I can't recall exactly what—"

"*You* dated *Bodin?*"

"Yes." Mrs. Doddard laughed. "Why sound so shocked?"

"You two are definitely poles apart."

"We weren't always. We both worked our way through college, although he quit when his father was stricken with cancer. So, Abner became the breadwinner. Paradise Village isn't New York City. We have no welfare programs."

"I'm not so sure *we* even have a city. But when I said poles apart, I didn't necessarily mean financially. Personality, intelligence, etc.—all are factors."

"Abner may not be an Einstein, but he certainly had drive in his day. Kept his nose to the proverbial grindstone in college and worked hard as a mechanic, too."

"Before I interrupted, you were explaining how you met Mr. Doddard."

"Oh, yes. I had stopped by to see Abner and

96

met Sam. He made his fortune by collecting a chain of body and fender shops throughout the nation. Abner introduced us and we found ourselves mutually attracted. We began to date, then shortly thereafter became engaged. Within a year we were married."

"From all the surrounding evidence"—I waved my arm about—"I'd assume you are extremely wealthy."

Mrs. Doddard smiled, glanced conspiratorially about, and shaded her mouth with her hand, whispering, "Filthy rich. Millions."

I laughed and said, "Glad to hear it. But tell me, why did you remain in Paradise Village?"

"Why not? I've traveled the world and never found a better place than this. Have you?"

"Well—I don't know yet—"

"Aside from this recent—business—I've always been happy here. At first Sam wanted to live in New York City, but when given the choice between the Statue of Liberty or me, he chose me. I'm warmer." We both laughed. She continued, "After a time, he grew to love it here. Even inconvenienced his business associates by holding meetings here instead of New York."

"I see. What was Sheriff Bodin's reaction to your leaving him for Mr. Doddard?"

"I didn't exactly leave him. I played the field and he was one of the fielders. But that's all. There was nothing serious between us. At first he seemed a bit disappointed, but he came to our wedding."

"Did he remain working for your husband?"

"Oh, yes. He used to joke about opening his own body and fender shop someday, but he became sheriff instead. So we kept our little monopoly here."

"There are no other garages?"

"Only gas stations. We do all the mechanical work for the village."

"What about engine work?"

"That, too. We started with body and fender work and eventually branched out into engines, too. However, we still keep the old B and F title. My husband had some sort of superstition about changing titles."

"Interesting. How about your other suitors? How did they react?"

"They all got over it. Not even one suicide to brag about."

I laughed and said, "Well, thanks for letting me take up so much of your time."

"I hope I've been of some help."

"I'm sure you have, though only time will tell for certain."

When I walked through her door, Robin greeted me with hands on hips, and eyes hard set. She said, "Well?"

"Well? Yes. I've never felt better."

"You're not very funny. What did *she* have to say?"

"Not much. Just a few declarative sentences. Take off your clothes. Get into bed. From there it was all moans and groans."

"Ha! Ha! You're a goddamn riot!" Robin turned her back to me, folded her arms, and stared at the ceiling. I placed my hands on her shoulders, but she shrugged them off. I said,

98

"Come on, silly. I went up there for investigative purposes only."

"How *deeply* did you investigate?"

"Not deeply enough to satisfy me. That's for sure."

Robin looked over her shoulder at me. "What do you mean?"

"I've been playing around with a theory, but I haven't found much evidence in its favor."

She turned completely around. "What kind of theory?"

"Well, it bugs me that first Mrs. Doddard loses her husband and then gets the priest's picture in the mail. The husband's murder is understandable inasmuch as it launched this terror campaign against the town. The priest's murder is understandable in the same context. But what the hell does he really gain by sending the priest's picture to Mrs. Doddard?"

"Shock value. It really shook everyone."

"The murder alone would have accomplished that. If it was the town he wanted to shock, he could have sent it to the newspapers or the mayor's office."

"I guess you're right. Although Doddard's murder was fresh in everyone's mind. Perhaps harassing the widow seemed more sensational to him."

"Maybe. But Father Moore was one of her beaus before entering the priesthood, you know."

"Really?"

"Uh-huh. Seems like somebody's trying to add insult to injury. Rub salt in her wounds."

"But why?"

"That is *the* question. I think I'd even give up sex to know the answer."

Robin's eyebrows arched. She said, "Really?"

"Yeah. For at least an hour."

I placed my hand on her neck and massaged it gently. Robin didn't shove me away, but she didn't exactly melt in my arms, either. I said, "Speaking of sex, what say we—"

"Sorry. I haven't paid my toll yet."

She went into the bedroom and came out counting a roll of bills. I said, "I'll drive you."

"No, thanks."

"Why not?"

"I feel like taking off by myself for a while. You just take off whenever you feel like it, don't you? Why can't I do the same?"

She marched out, hopped her bike, and pedaled away. I started to make a drink but changed my mind. I paced back and forth until I caught a glimpse of my reflection in one of the window-panes. What the hell was a forty-two-year-old ex-cop doing mooning about like a love-struck fifteen-year-old? I blamed it on the atmosphere. Too much sun, surf, and murder. There was only one solution. Retire to a saloon and grow old with dignity.

Adolph shook my hand and said, "Ooh, it's so good to see you, Mr. Callahan. What are you drinking?"

"Large beer."

"Where have you been hiding the past few days, for heaven's sake?"

"Here and there. What's new?"

Adolph gestured disgustedly toward the TV. "Nothing but this."

The television was focused on the proceedings

at Town Hall. People stood in line single file, with sealed and signed, cash-filled packets in their hands. Before dropping the money into the sack, they held it up to the cameras for inspection. A commentator droned on about the proceedings, which were self-explanatory, anyway. I turned back to Adolph and said, "How's Charley been these days?"

"Oh, you know that Charley. In again, out again. Though lately he's been spending money."

"Really?"

"Oh, yes. Last night he got drunk on whiskey. Good stuff, too. Must've spent seventeen dollars plus my fifty-cent tip. Hmmph!"

"Seventeen dollars? And a tip, no less? What'd he do, mug someone with his armpits?"

Adolph laughed and said, "Ooh! You're so quick! You should have been a comedian."

"I was. The laughingstock of New York's Finest."

I meant that remark as a joke but felt a twinge of regret as soon as I said it. Adolph said, "Stop! For heaven's sake. My sides are killing me."

I spent the rest of the sfternoon nursing beer and swapping jokes with Adolph. Business came in spurts. Clusters of people would enter, usually after having paid their dues, and talk in tones of anger or relief. After a couple of drinks, they'd usually leave, only to be replaced by a similar group.

During the course of the day my thoughts strayed occasionally to Robin. I wondered if she had returned home, and, if so, was she thinking about me? Was she waiting or looking for me? I doubted the latter. I'm not so hard to find. Was she still moody? Probably. Then my thoughts turned to Mrs. Doddard. Now there was a woman with charm. Ideas floated through my mind that stung my conscience.

An announcement from the TV erased these unsavory thoughts. I glanced up and saw three very familiar people on the screen. Mayor Hanlon stood in the center, flanked on one side by Robin and on the other by the autograph seeker who had nearly loosened the foundation of my bungalow. The sheriff was saying, "Miss Robin Blair has graciously volunteered to deliver the—ahem—toll money according to the instructions received. I'm gratified to note the spirit among the scores of our young boys who volunteered to go along with Miss Blair. However, on her recommendation we have accepted Herbie Dorfus, the courageous son of our respected high school principal, Dwight Dorfus. With Mr. Dorfus's kind permission, of course." Halfhearted clapping and muted vocal encouragement echoed from the crowd.

Adolph said, "My, oh my! What do you think of that?"

"I can sum it up in one word," I said. "Bullshit!"

Town Hall was packed. My shouts of, "Officer Callahan, police business," and the fact that my face was well known, enabled me to worm my way up to the telephone-lined tables where Robin, Herbie, and all the town officials sat. The black phones were constantly ringing, causing nerve problems for the town officials as they hurriedly answered them. Only the hot line, a conspicuous red instrument, was silent. Its number was unknown to the public since it was to be used

only for emergency calls between town officials.
I ignored the greetings of the mayor and the
sheriff and spoke directly to Robin.

"Just what the hell do you think you're doing?"

She closed her eyes indignantly and said, "I'm
driving up with the money. Herbie's accompanying me."

"Herbie! Great protection!"

"I chose him because he's levelheaded."

"How come you were picked and not someone
else?"

"Because"—Robin opened her eyes—"when
the killer first announced his terms I called
Sheriff Bodin and made him promise to give the
job to me."

I shot Bodin a glance not reserved for bathing
beauties. He looked away. I turned back to Robin
and said, "Do you think this is a game? You know
what's being planned—"

She pressed a finger to her lips, looked about,
and said, "Shh!"

"Shh, my ass!" I said, but lowered my voice.
"If Edison muffs this, you and the kid might pay
the price."

"It's a chance I want to take. I must take it.
Think of the publicity."

"Publicity? You talk like a budding actress, for
Christ's sake!"

"You don't understand. If Edison's plan works,
I'll be a heroine. Especially when the people find
out that I was informed of the plan from the start.
Everyone will come to my parlor."

"Your parlor?" I began to wonder about Robin,
though she looked sane enough. "Your parlor?"

"I told you I intended to go into business,

didn't I? I've got just enough capital saved to start. And after this my credit will be unlimited, anyway. I'll have no trouble opening my own beauty parlor."

"No wonder you were so anxious to get me involved in the case." I locked eyes with her. "If I cracked it, you'd share in the glory."

"It's time to go, Robin," Bodin interrupted. "The money's all collected."

Robin turned toward Bodin, who was carrying the sackful of loot. The cheers and shouts of encouragement from the crowd brightened her features. By the time she reached the door, she was beaming. When Bodin returned, I said, "How long will this whole thing take?"

"Robin should be back in about an hour and a half. There's nothing to do till then."

"See you later."

I felt kind of depressed as I sat at the table studying the route she was to follow on the sheriff's map. Some of the people drifted back to their homes or elsewhere. The mayor sat at a table conversing with various politicians and reporters. Bodin stood alone in a corner sipping coffee from a cardboard container. The earlier din of the telephones had ceased.

I must have lost myself in thought because I nearly leaped out of my seat when a roar went up from the crowd, followed by cheers and applause. Robin and Herbie strode through the front door. She looked excited and happy. He calmly sucked a lollipop. I exhaled in relief. At that exact moment, the red hot line rang. Bodin snatched it up and asked who was there. Then his face tightened. He slowly lowered the receiver. Then he bent over and whispered into the mayor's ear. The mayor's face grew whiter than the belly of a fish. He muttered something like, "Oh, my God!"

Robin stopped by the table and placed her hand on mine. She said, "Marty—please—try to understand. I—I really like you. Just for yourself. I do."

Herbie was being congratulated by the townsfolk and embraced by his father, who could barely get his arms around him. The mayor was sweating and Bodin was shaking his head. Mayor Hanlon said something and Bodin half ran out to the street. I said to Robin, "I think your efforts were wasted."

"What? Why?"

"If I'm not mistaken, Bodin's racing up to All Hallow's Point for the money you left there. I'll bet that call he got was from the killer."

"God!" Robin's hand flew to her mouth. She mumbled through it, "My God!"

The mayor waited about twenty minutes, giving Bodin a good head start, before making this announcement:

"Citizens of Paradise Village. I—I have just received dreadful news. This—this assassin has phoned, claiming—quite falsely—that we—my administration and the sheriff's office conspired to sabotage tonight's mission. This is a total falsehood. This—this devil is obviously looking for an excuse to raise the ransom—the Death Toll as he calls it. He has vowed to take another life. If he does, it is out of sheer malice. We have acted in good faith. We—"

I grabbed the mayor's padded shoulder and shoved him. He staggered sideways, nearly falling. I spoke into the microphone.

"Ladies and gentlemen! Your mayor is a goddamn liar!"

A hush fell over the crowd. The mayor ordered me arrested. Two uniformed deputies pinned my arms behind my back. Their big mistake was in not covering my mouth. I continued, "Your mayor, who wants so badly to be your governor, positioned a state cop named Edison as a sniper at All Hallow's Point—"

The police tightened their grip, and sharp pains in my shoulders and back cut short my speech. Someone shouted, "Let him talk!" Another said, "Let go of him." I looked back at the two men, who were glancing nervously at each other, and said, "Better release me before you two become memories."

They took my advice. I positioned myself before the mike and said, "Your mayor backed the plan of state police Captain Edison to shoot down the killer sniper style. I disagreed with the plan but to no avail. Now the ante has doubled, and some-one—one of you—will die."

A folding chair shot through the air and bounced off the table. A wave of angry people surged forward. Tables were overturned and more chairs flew. I heard the tinkle of breaking glass as I looked about for Mayor Hanlon. He was gone, but a side door was swinging. I walked through it and saw the taillights of a car retreating in the distance. Behind me I heard shouts and screams coupled with wrenching, breaking, and tearing sounds. Robin appeared beside me.

She clasped my right hand with both of hers and said, "Come home with me?"

"Good-bye, Robin." I looked away, laughed without pleasure, and said, "And good-bye to Paradise."

Chapter Nine

The following morning I stood beneath a hot shower and brooded about the way Robin had tried to use me. But when I compared her to Amanda, I realized I hadn't fared badly. After all, Amanda had given me as little as possible and had taken as much as she could. I believe her goal in life had been to bring back debtor's prison, with me as its first occupant. She had insisted on our buying a home I couldn't afford, in a neighborhood I didn't like, and furnishing it in a style that kept my creditors smiling.

Even after we separated, she kept her hand in my pocket. I had to get shot to convince her to divorce me. My little fib about *having* to retire at half pay was the clincher. It prodded her to spring the trap on some businessman she had been dating. Last I heard, they were married.

Robin, on the other hand, gave a lot without really taking anything from me. Still, her intentions were deceitful. I guess that's what hurt.

My thoughts turned to Paradise Village itself, my conflict with the mayor's son, and all these murders. It gave me a feeling of relief to know I was returning to crime-ridden New York City.

Stepping out of the shower, I dried myself off, wrapped a towel around my hips, and entered the kitchen. I wasn't very hungry, so I just brewed a pot of coffee. My first sip was followed by a knock on the door. I cursed under my breath and growled, "Who is it?"

"Sheriff Bodin."

"Just a minute."

I opened the door and let him squeeze in. His face was the color of a broiled lobster, and his bloodshot eyes twitched nervously. He said, "I'm sorry to have to disturb you, Mr. Callahan."

"That makes two of us." I gestured toward the pot on the stove. "Coffee?"

"Got anything stronger?"

"There's beer in the refrigerator, and"—I pointed to the kitchen cabinet—"you'll find all kinds of knockout drops in there."

Bodin filled a water glass halfway with rye, drained it, and poured another. He said, "They were—they were gonna skin me alive."

"Who?"

"The people. The only thing that saved me was telling them that I opposed the mayor's plan and even brought you to his house to talk him out of it. That's when they asked—I should say ordered—me to see you."

"See me? What for?"

"They figured that we—that we're friends and I'd have the best chance of persuadin' you to take this—this thing over."

"Forget it. I'm packing it in today."

"Leaving?"

"And how. Paradise Village is one place I hope never to see again."

"Would you reconsider?" Bodin finished his drink and poured another. "Please?"

"No way."

"But think of the people—"

"The people, eh? Know why I retired, Sheriff?"

"I—uh—gathered it was for health reasons."

"That's what I wanted everyone to believe. Actually, I retired because I got sick of serving *the people*. My partner was killed during that famous raid, leaving a wife and three kids behind. For what, Sheriff? For what?"

"I—I know how you must feel. What with the heroin havin' been stolen out of police headquarters and all. But—"

"Seven pounds of it. Replaced with sugar. Probably before my partner was cold in his grave."

"I know. That was bad."

"I'll tell you something worse. The day I left the hospital, I was trying to hail a cab when I heard two truck drivers talking about someone who hit big on the numbers game. They were lamenting their own lousy luck. A few days later, I listened to a bartender telling one of his customers where to buy bootleg cigarettes. This type of thing is common, even though everybody knows the profits go to organized crime where they're reinvested into narcotics as well as everything else. These are the people who scream about law and morality. As far as I'm concerned, *the people* deserve what they get."

"Including your partner's wife and children?"

"Huh?"

"They're people, too."

The townspeople stood en masse on Main Street. They cheered, saluted, and thumped the sheriff's car in comradely fashion as he inched it through them. Dozens of hands slapped my back as I edged my way to the top step of Town Hall. All its windows were shattered. I could imagine what the interior looked like. Bodin was handed a bullhorn by one of his deputies. He passed it to me.

Although it was a clear, bright morning, the sun wasn't strong enough to blind me to the fear-ridden expressions on the people's faces. I recognized some of them. Adolph stood up front, nodding his head like one of those toy dogs you see in the rear windows of some cars. Robin was pressed more deeply within the crowd. Her expression seemed to radiate excitement rather than fear.

News photographers snapped stills or shot moving pictures, while reporters, armed with tape recorders and notepads, waited attentively. Several new faces, some familiar, appeared among the reporters. Aaron Farmer looked detached but attentive. I tried to speak but only grunted. A hush fell over the crowd. Aside from the whirring of a small aircraft high above and the flapping of the Stars and Stripes on the Town Hall flagpole, silence prevailed. I said, "Ladies and gentlemen, I'm addressing you on behalf of Sheriff Bodin in order to clear up a few misconceptions. First off—let me state this emphatically—Sheriff Bodin definitely did oppose the double cross formulated by state police Captain Edison and Mayor Hanlon."

Cheers and applause greeted this statement.

111

Bodin wiped his brow and smiled in relief. I continued: "The Sheriff engaged my assistance in opposing their plan, but to no avail."

Someone—the voice sounded female—shouted, "Why didn't you tell us before it went into effect?"

A grumble arose from the crowd. I said, "I am not now, and never was, officially connected with this case. My advice was asked for and I gave it. Perhaps I should have exposed their plan, but then the killer probably would have felt double-crossed, anyway. My only hope was to abort it from the start. When I failed to do so, the only other alternative that made sense to me was to say nothing and hope the plan would work."

The grumble had been replaced by the hum of muted voices. I assumed they accepted my explanation. I added icing to the cake by saying, "When the plan failed, I felt duty-bound to reveal the truth to you."

More cheers and applause. Now was the time to tell them the bad news. While it was true Bodin's argument touched me, he didn't reach deeply enough to make me change my stand. I said, "Ladies and gentlemen, Sheriff Bodin has requested, on your behalf, that I assume charge of this—uh—situation, and—"

A thunderous ovation drowned me out. I waited, then said, "I—don't know quite how to say this—but—I'm afraid I can't accept the sheriff's—or rather your—offer."

Their silent response was unnerving. Aaron Farmer elbowed his way up the steps and shouted, "Why are you refusing to help, sir?"

"Personal reasons."

"But what could be more important than the saving of human lives?"

"Farmer, my decision stands. I'll thank you not to ask any more loaded questions. Ladies and gentlemen, my advice to you is to place this case in Sheriff Bodin's hands. His thinking is along the same lines as my own, and I'm confident he is more than qualified to handle the situation. I recommend him, and now I'm turning this meeting over to him."

I lowered the horn and said to Bodin, "I softened them up for you. Now appeal to the killer for new instructions. Pledge to deal honestly, and then hope."

"Yes, Mr. Callahan. I sure will! Thank you! Thank you!"

The anxiety that had tightened his features earlier was fading. He shook my hand vigorously, signaled to one of his deputies, and said, "Drive Mr. Callahan home."

The crowd parted for me as I descended the steps. Their expressions and murmurings indicated disappointment. But I wasn't about to worry. I was putting it all behind me.

My mood lightened as I packed. I decided a parting drink would be in order. As I poured it, a light, feminine tapping sounded on my door. I hoped, but didn't really believe, that it would be someone other than Robin. I wanted to leave without unpleasantness, but I braced myself and said, "Come in."

The door opened slowly, and Robin, beautiful in a demure white dress, entered. She cast her eyes down and practically whispered, "You're really leaving?"

"Yes."

For an awkard moment neither of us spoke. Then I said, "Sit down."

"Thank you."

Demure or not, the dress accented every curve as she gently lowered herself onto the sofa. I said, "Like a drink?"

"Soda's fine."

I filled a glass and handed it to her. After we both sipped our drinks, she said, "I want you to know—I'll miss you. . . ."

Robin's voice sputtered out in a choke. I stared silently at my drink while she composed herself. This was exactly the situation I had hoped to avoid. Finally, she said, "I don't blame you for feeling hurt. I did use you—it's true—but—"

"Forget it. We both had a fling. What's done is done."

"No! I can't let you leave without knowing the truth. I saw an opportunity and grabbed it. I had hoped you would crack the case so I could share in the glory, true. That's why I prodded you on. But—that's not all. I never had sex with anyone—voluntarily, that is—until I met you. I—I don't know if I love you, but—but you are very special . . ."

Tears glimmered in Robin's eyes as she gripped my free hand with one of hers. She pressed her face against my knuckles and whimpered. I put my glass down, caressed her neck, and said, "Take it easy. Chin up, now."

She sniffed, wiped her eyes with the handker-

chief I offered, and blew her nose. I said,
"Feeling better?"

She nodded just as another light tapping
sounded on my door. We eyed each other quizzically. I shrugged and said, "Come in."

Mrs. Doddard, chic in a black pantsuit, glided
into the room. She smiled a greeting at Robin,
then extended her hand to me and said, "Good
afternoon, Mr. Callahan. I'm sorry for this intrusion, but—"

"No intrusion at all," I said quickly. "Sit down,
please."

"Thank you."

"Drink?"

"No, thanks. I—I've come here to discuss some
important business with you."

"Oh?"

Robin, glaring sullenly at Mrs. Doddard, stood
up and said, "Well, I guess I'd better be going."

Mrs. Doddard reached over, squeezed Robin's
hand, and said, "Please don't leave on my account,
dear. This concerns you just as much as the rest
of us."

Robin sat down again. Mrs. Doddard said, "My
reason for coming here, Mr. Callahan, is to try
to persuade you not to leave. I—I'd like to hire
you to remain with us—the villagers—that is, until
this—uh—problem is solved."

"But why? Sheriff Bodin can do the same things
I would do."

"Although his intentions are sincere, I'm afraid
the people of Paradise, myself included, have very
little confidence in his ability. As a sheriff, I think
he's a very good car mechanic."

"Car mechanic?" Robin said, looking puzzled.

115

I laughed and said, "That's what he was before becoming sheriff."

"Oh."

"Mrs. Doddard," I said, "I might agree with you on that score."

"So might the killer, which could be disastrous. Besides, I'm hoping—I suppose—that somehow an experienced detective like you might come across something that could. . . ."

She left the sentence unfinished. Robin said, "I'm afraid Marty's awfully stubborn when his mind's made up, Mrs. Doddard."

"I loved my husband," Mrs. Doddard said quickly. "I want his killer caught. Please stay. I'll pay anything you ask."

Sorrow seems to cast people into a common mold. Mrs. Doddard in no way resembled my dead partner's wife, yet, for a moment, she might have been her twin. I said, "If I stay, the killer gets paid because stopping these murders is more important than anything else, even catching him."

Mrs. Doddard nodded earnestly. "I agree."

"And I must tell you I really don't think there's a very good chance of catching him."

"Any chance is enough. Will you accept my offer?"

"Yes."

"You mean you'll stay?" Robin asked, looking surprised and annoyed.

"Yes."

Mrs. Doddard drew a checkbook from her purse and said, "How much—uh—"

"I wouldn't dream of taking your money."

Mrs. Doddard was at a loss for words. Finally, she shook my hand and thanked me. I assured

116

her I would contact the sheriff and announce my plans publicly for the killer's benefit. After she left, I said to Robin, "Guess I may as well call Bodin."

"You may as well is right. We wouldn't want Mrs. Doddard to think her influence is waning already."

I ignored that. The operator tried several different lines until she reached Bodin. I informed him of my decision and gave him some instructions. He sounded surprised but told me to meet him at Town Hall as soon as I could. Robin decided, not too cheerfully, to join me. As we walked out of the house together, someone said, "Hello, Callahan!"

The glare of the sun caused me to blink several times. My eyes adjusted to the sight of Burton Hanlon and his ever-present companions, the Pagan brothers. Hanlon was striking the palm of his left hand with his right fist. I said, "Can you flip a half dollar like George Raft?"

"You're cute with the mouth, Callahan. That's why my father's career is all screwed up. I'm going to close that cute mouth of yours."

I nudged Robin away from me. She took the hint.

"Gentlemen, please," I said, throwing my hands up in protest, "Let's be reasonable about—"

I finished my sentence with a hard kick to Hanlon's groin. The toe of my shoe landed squarely on target. He crumpled with barely a grunt. Both brothers followed their leader's descent with shock-widened eyes. By the time it dawned on these not-quite geniuses that they should be watching me instead of Hanlon, it was too late.

My left hand, fingers arched, raked one brother's eyes while my elbow found a home in the other's throat. One man clutched his throat, danced and gagged. The other cupped his face with both hands and screamed. A chop to the back of the neck ended all the screaming. Robin, eyes bugging, said, "Is—is that karate?"

"Nope! That's Brooklyn. Greenpoint, to be exact." I glanced at the two inert figures and their dancing companion and said, "I don't think these gentlemen will mind if we leave them to each other. Look what they have in common."

By the time we reached town, the news of my change of heart had spread like the peal of a church bell on a quiet Sunday morning. Caesar returning victorious to Rome couldn't have received a better reception than I did. As I inched my car through the crowd, the people waved, shouted, and thumped it with even more gusto than they had originally. My back and shoulders were sore from friendly slaps by the time I reached the top steps of Town Hall.

A long table, complete with microphones, had been set up in my absence. I was ushered by Bodin to the center of the table and seated before a mike. He sat beside me and announced to the applauding crowd that I had graciously reconsidered and was taking charge of the ransom problem. Then he turned the meeting over to me. I said:

"Ladies and gentlemen. By now I'm sure you're all aware of my opinion regarding this— ah—Death Toll that has been levied on Paradise Village. From the start I affirmed that it should be paid. Now I want to state emphatically to the *Toll Collector* that I am awaiting instructions. Tell me how much you want and how you want it delivered. I will remain in Town Hall until midnight, and then, because of the destruction inside, return home to sleep. I will return here at nine A.M. tomorrow and repeat this vigil. I can be reached at either place at these numbers."

I read off my home number and several others for Town Hall, then reaffirmed my own and the villagers' willingness to cooperate. The people shouted their approval. I instructed them to return to their homes and explained that any new developments would be reported immediately through the media. This seemed to satisfy them because they began to disperse almost at once. The killer could hardly fail to notice their eagerness to cooperate. I felt pretty certain that their attitude would suffice to prevent any more deaths.

Hell, was I wrong!

I spent the rest of the day among the semiruins of Town Hall drinking coffee and fencing verbally with reporters. They were curious to know what had brought about my change of heart and seemed amused when I mentioned the word *conscience*. Midnight came without any contact from the killer, so I called it a night and went home. Robin sat quietly beside me throughout the journey but offered, after we parked outside her house, to spend part or all of the night with me. My body said yes, but my common sense said no. I explained that with the press keeping tabs on me, our little affair could become a circus. She accepted my explanation with a nod but no com-

119

ment and turned her cheek to me as I kissed her goodnight. As she walked away, I distinctly felt a chapter of my life coming to a close.

After breakfast the following morning, I phoned Robin and asked if she'd care to join me at Town Hall. She answered negatively. A little while later, as I parked in town, I noticed there were fewer people out than usual. Bodin and an array of reporters were on hand at Town Hall while workmen salvaged and repaired the damage. Bodin shook my hand, sent one of his deputies to get me a container of coffee, and said, "Heard the news?"

"What news?"

"Mayor Hanlon's at the capital"—he winked on that note—"briefing the governor on the situation."

"I think he'd better stay there awhile."

"I think he intends to."

The deputy returned with my coffee. I took my first sip as another uniformed officer entered and strode briskly toward us. He stopped in front of our table and handed Bodin a white envelope. The deputy's hand was shaking. Bodin frowned and said, "Who's watching the office, Dick?"

Dick's complexion resembled newly stirred ashes. He said, "Nobody—"

"Nobody! Suppose—"

"Abner! Please!" The deputy looked around warily; his voice dropped to a whisper. "I found this in the box with the rest of the mail. It was placed there. Not postmarked. Just read it. Please!"

Again the deputy glanced cautiously about. The reporters and cameramen, a dozen or so in all, were passing their tedious vigil drinking coffee in clutches or playing penny-ante poker. None seemed to take particular notice of the deputy. The sheriff opened the envelope, extracted the letter, and read its contents. Breathing deeply, he handed the letter to me. It was composed like the first one, its lettering formed by cut strips of paper. It said:

INSTRUCTIONS WILL BE FOUND IN MARTY CALLAHAN'S BUNGALOW!

The hairs on the back of my neck began to quiver. Aaron Farmer, whose natural instinct for news must have been aroused, excused himself from the poker game and sauntered over. He said, "Something up?"

Bodin looked from Farmer to me. I said, "Yeah. We just heard from the killer."

Sandwiched front and rear by two police cars, and accompanied by Bodin, I drove back to my bungalow. Our entourage was completed by a van in the rear filled with newsmen. When we arrived, I found the door to my bungalow unlocked. Bodin's hand rested on the butt of his pistol as we entered. I immediately noticed a small portable tape recorder lying on my coffee table. A strip of white tape adhering to its side bore the name *Reverend John A. Moore*.

One of Bodin's troops did a quick check of my rooms while the other two attempted vainly to stall the reporters outside. I told the cops to stop wasting their time, instructed the reporters to sit down and shut up, then flicked on the recorder.

121

It wasn't the message on the tape, it was the voice that made me shudder.

"Mr. Callahan," the voice said, "I'm—I'm givin' ya this message in my own words. Fact is—that— the ransom—uh—Death Toll was doubled because of the mayor's double cross. It's to be delivered tonight at midnight. Same place as before. Money's to be got together in Town Hall same way— before TV and everything. Like last time. This time it's to be delivered by Robin and Sheriff Bodin, since Bodin seems so sincere. Besides, what better way is there to protect money from hijackers than a police guard? Bodin is to stay in the car while Robin delivers. Because of—Collector's fai—faith in your word—only—only—" Sobs garbled the voice at this point. The audible clicks of the tape recorder being shut off and then on again followed. "Because—faith—only unimportant citizen—dies—this time—my God!"

The tape finished on that note. I glanced at the mummified expressions of my companions and said, "The killer's murdered Charley Fetters."

We reached Charley's home in record time. He was lying beneath blood-soaked sheets with his throat slashed. Someone opened the window and the crisp, salty air kept me from retching. Bodin ordered us not to touch anything until he got a fingerprint expert from the state police.

I wandered about, hands in pockets, looking for God knows what. The only thing I spotted was a gray tail protruding limply from beneath the ancient tub in the bathroom. Next to the tub was a large bowl with just a little foam in it. I got down on my knees, reached under the tub, and

122

pulled the creature out. He hung in my hand, eyes closed, and burped. Bodin stuck his head in and said, "Find anything?"

"You wouldn't believe what I found."

Chapter Ten

My inebriated feline friend slept soundly on the
front seat beside me as I drove back to Town Hall.
This time my police escort consisted of only one
car, Bodin having kept the rest of his force at
Charley's apartment to await the lab technician.
My first thought upon coasting to a halt was to let
the cat remain in my car. But the thought of his
waking up in a strange place with a bladder full
of beer made me change my mind. So I carried
him inside with me. One of the deputies dug up
a pillow upon which I tucked the cat, placing him
in a corner of the room. Then I sent the deputy
out for cat litter, cat food, and a six-pack.

Three of the newsmen had returned in the police car while the others stayed with Bodin. Everyone concerned agreed it would be best for me to
announce Charley's death immediately and rally
the villagers to Town Hall for the final collection.
First I called Robin, who eagerly agreed to the
instructions. Then, as soon as the equipment was
set up, I made my announcement, explaining that
details of Charley's death would be issued later.
The response wasn't long in coming.

Once again the cameras rolled, recording the tribute being paid by terrified citizens to the tune of one million dollars. Seeing the people reduced to spiritless robots was disheartening, and the long hours of sitting around with nothing to do turned my sour mood totally black. After a while, the cat woke up and looked about with puzzled eyes. I petted him and after a few strokes he purred. Next, I placed him in a box of cat litter, which he put to expert use. Finally, I instructed a deputy to take him into one of the back rooms for a beer. Away from the cameras. I had enough problems without tangling with the animal protection societies.

Robin appeared during the latter part of the evening. Her body was molded into white pants and a blue halter. She was braless, of course. Immediately, the reporters swamped her.

Was she frightened?

Yes. But determined to go through with this.

What were her plans for the future?

To open a beauty salon.

Where?

Paradise Village, of course. It's her home, isn't it?

Did she have a locale picked?

Several in mind.

So on and on went the interview, with Robin basking in the electronic eyes of the cameras and the admiring eyes of her blackmailed fellow villagers. Bodin returned a little later and drew some attention from her. He explained that the state police were still dusting for fingerprints. The last citizen paid up at eleven fifteen, which left Robin forty-five minutes more of coverage. She fluttered from reporter to reporter, overly attentive, exceptionally gracious. Her attention focused on everyone but me.

Midnight came, and Robin and Bodin went. This time two sacks were required, so I carried one. The press accompanied us to the car and recorded their departure. I told one of the deputies to get the remainder of the six-pack from the refrigerator in the kitchen and offer the beer out. But since the cat was asleep, and no one else accepted any, I drank alone. Which was just as well, considering I wasn't in the mood to be sociable. The idea of a sophisticated savage reducing a town of law-abiding citizens to a frightened pack stuck in my craw.

Images of Doddard's charred, lifeless body cropped up in my mind. Kill a man to prove a point. What about the sorrow of his loved ones? But savages don't care about such things. I recalled Mrs. Doddard's courageous suffering. The vicious act of furthering her torture with Father Moore's picture annoyed me like a back itch that couldn't quite be reached to scratch. Reflecting upon Mrs. Doddard made the wheels of my mind stop on our last conversation. The one that had so annoyed Robin.

Poor Robin!

Raped, humiliated, and nearly framed to look like a whore. *Framed!* Another word that knocked my emotions awry. Who the hell did all the bastards of the world think they were? My silent question was interrupted by Robin's and Bodin's return. I sat at the table long enough to hear them announce that the instructions had been adhered to and nothing had gone amiss. Then, as

Robin described her feelings while traipsing through the woods with the money, I ducked into the room containing my cat, scooped him up, found an exit, and ducked out. I inhaled the salty night air, and my furry partner did likewise. I thought about the Lighthouse with its cold-beer tap and said, "Obnoxious, old buddy, I know where we can get the real stuff."

He meowed in a tone that struck me as positive, so off we went.

Business in the Lighthouse was anything but positive. Adolph was the only soul there. His eyes shifted from the TV to me and the cat as we entered. He scratched his hump, rocked his head, and said, "So good to see you, Mr. Callahan. I've just been listening to Robin and the sheriff. I guess the ordeal is over, huh?"

"I hope so. Dewar's on the rocks—double—and a large beer. I'll take some suds for the cat, too."

I placed Obnoxious on the bar. Adolph laughed and said, "Charley's cat?"

"Until today."

"Thought I recognized him."

Adolph served me first, which made the cat howl with indignation. Then he placed a bowlful of beer on the bar, into which my cat's head disappeared. Between the lapping, purring, and gargling sounds he made, I wasn't sure if he was drinking or drowning. Adolph said, "Poor Charley."

"Yeah. Poor Charley. Poor Sam Doddard. Poor Mrs. Doddard. Poor Father Moore. Poor Robin. Poor everybody. Poor me."

I drained the booze and sipped the beer. Adolph

127

continued, "Yes—everybody involved is certainly unfortunate, but—Charley—well—for the first time in his life things seemed to be picking up."

"How so?"

"I told you he had plenty of spending money the other night, right?"

"Yeah. Come to think of it, you did."

"Well—he could be so silly when he wanted to be—you know?"

"Yeah. So? What are you getting at?"

"Well, he kept flashing his roll around—"

"Just—just a minute. How much would you say he had on him?"

"Oh, about thirty dollars."

"That's a roll?"

Even the cat stopped drinking and looked at Adolph as though awaiting an explanation.

"It was for Charley."

"Did he say where it came from?"

"He dropped sly hints about having a secret benefactor. Working on a secret deal with someone. That's all I know."

"And now he's dead."

"Yes. Poor soul."

"I thought you didn't like him."

"We had our differences, but everyone has the right to live."

"Give me another drink."

"The cat, too?"

Obnoxious burped. I said, "He's had enough."

I sipped my fresh round in silence. My cat licked his lips and purred. Adolph switched channels and focused his attention on a horror story. So did I. But not the same one. Who was Charley's

128

secret benefactor? The killer? Would a guy like Charley, who helped a stranger like me, knowingly aid a killer? For money, perhaps? If so, what kind of help could he actually be? What could he do? Or was this all a big coincidence? Did he just find or win some money and make up this mysterious secret? The more questions I asked myself, the more confused I became. I decided to try another line of reasoning, but not until I'd had another round. I said, "Adolph, shake up the molecules. I'm starting to rust."

Adolph did his duty to my drinking glasses, and I did my duty to his drinks. I thought back to the first killing. Doddard. Explosion. Then Father Moore. Tortured. Mrs. Doddard gets picture. Possible link there. Charley's death. No link at all. Chain broken. Try again. Doddard. Explosion. Could be done by anyone with basic knowledge of explosives. Father Moore. Tortured. No sign of forcible entry into his home. My cottage. Entered. No sign of forcible entry. The killer must be someone who had been trusted by the victims. Someone familiar enough to gain access almost anywhere without raising suspicion. Perhaps someone with a motive for revenge as well as profit.

An electric tingle surged up my spine. My hands grew cold, my palms damp. A totally unrelated thought entered my mind like an odd piece of puzzle. Yet it seemed to fit. My wet fingers had trouble gripping a dime that lay on the bar. I walked over to the pay phone and dialed a number. After a few rings, a familiar female voice said, "Hello?"

"Mrs. Doddard, this is Marty Callahan. I'm sorry to disturb you so late—"

129

"It's quite all right. I've been watching television. Can't sleep with all this excitement. Is anything wrong?"

"No. It's—it's just that a question has suddenly entered my mind that—uh—might be important to the outcome of this case."

"Oh?"

"Do you remember when Robin Blair's father was killed several years ago? The car crash?"

"Why, yes. I do."

"Did your husband's garage inspect the wreck to determine the accident's cause?"

"I suppose s—no! I remember now."

"Why not?"

"There was no need to. Sheriff Bodin took a very personal interest in the accident. He inspected the car himself."

"Himself?"

"Yes. Of course, as you know, he was quite capable."

"Yes. Quite." I thanked her and hung up the phone.

I thanked her very much indeed.

I brought the cat home, then drove over to Robin's house. Although it was nearly 3:00 A.M., her living-room light was on. My knock brought her to the door, bright-eyed and smiling. The smile quivered slightly as she said, "Oh! It's you!"

"You were expecting Robert Redford?"

"I—come in. I thought it might be more newspeople."

"Sorry to disappoint you."

"Drink?"

130

"Scotch and soda." I flopped on the sofa and waited for my drink. It wasn't long in coming. I saluted Robin, who didn't have a drink, and said, "Cheers."

She dimmed the living-room light and turned on soft music. I said, "Atmosphere and whiskey. What more can a man want?"

Robin sat down beside me and said, "Tell me. What more can a man want?"

I nuzzled her cheek with my nose and said, "Information."

"Information?" She looked puzzled. "What kind of information?"

"Exactly how did you and Bodin deliver the money?"

"How? You already know—"

I cut her story short with a shake of my head. "I know what you told the press, but did you really walk alone into the woods with the money while Bodin waited in the car?"

Robin looked wary. She said, "What are you driving at?"

"Those bags weighed eighty or ninety pounds apiece. Quite a job for a lady. Even if it was done in two trips."

"You—you won't tell the press?"

"I wouldn't dream of spoiling your image."

"I—I was afraid to go into the woods alone, so Sheriff Bodin brought the money to the designated area himself."

"You didn't go with him?"

"No." Robin looked away. "I—I felt safer sitting in the car with the engine running."

"Was it your idea or his that you remain behind?"

131

"Mine. I was scared."

"Are you certain it was yours, or did he—perhaps—suggest you might be in danger?"

"Well"—Robin closed her eyes and frowned—"he—when I mentioned being frightened—he—come to think of it—he did suggest I stay behind. I—"

I held up my hand to stop her from talking. There isn't much traffic in or around Paradise Village at three in the morning, so when a car passed by, I picked its sound right up. I could have sworn it slowed up outside the house. I walked over to the window, opened it, and looked out. A pair of red taillights retreated in the distance. Robin said, "What's wrong?"

I shrugged.

"Why are you asking all these questions?"

"Habit. Twenty years on the force and all that. You saw Bodin take the bags from the trunk?"

"Yes."

"From inside the car you could see this?"

"Yes, Marty. I saw the bags!"

"And you saw him take them into the woods?"

"Yes. I saw him take them into the woods."

"Thanks. That's all I wanted to know."

Robin placed a hand on my shoulder and said, "Surely—surely you don't suspect—Sheriff Bodin?"

"No! No!" I tried to sound nonchalant. "I just like to get all the details wrapped up. After all, even though any chances of catching this killer are pretty much out the window, there's no harm in thinking things out."

Robin yawned, so I wished her goodnight. I

132

made no advances and she made no offers. One thought kept rolling across my mind.

She saw him carry two bags into the woods. That didn't mean a damn thing!

Chapter Eleven

I left Robin's house feeling more sober than when I arrived. Bodin could have substituted bags. He could have had bags hidden in the grass by the edge of the road. If so, then everything added up and the killer was practically in the palm of my hand. The only thing missing was a little tangible called proof. As I drove through the clear, starlit night, I mapped out my next move. Obviously, I had to locate the money. Now, where could it be? Hidden in the woods? Definitely not. Too much danger from people and even animals.

Bodin probably substituted bags before entering the woods. The substituted bags might still be there. Not likely, but worth checking out, anyway. My next thought was that he must have left them hidden inside the police car trunk. Most unlikely. One of his men might find them. Not to mention the possibility of an accident. How about his house? Good possibility. Who the hell in Paradise Village would ever dream of searching the sheriff's house? I suddenly realized I didn't even know where Bodin lived. After pinpointing that information, all I'd have to do would be figure out how to gain access to his house.

Simple, yes?

Since my cottage had a phone, it also had a directory. I looked up Bodin's address, then spent the remaining wee hours drinking coffee. At sunup I drove out to the wooded area where Robin and Bodin had rendezvoused with the money. The thick green foliage glistened with dew, and a fresh mint aroma scented the air. Birds chirped gaily while I trudged painfully through thorny thickets and bushes. I reached Hangman's Tree after stumbling and falling only two or three times. A thorough search of the area convinced me that if substitute bags had been left behind, they were gone now.

I returned to town, stopped in a diner for breakfast, then drove out to Bodin's house. His house was old, whitewashed, and surrounded by woods. The nearest neighbor was about half a mile away. Although his garage door was closed, I saw no sign of life within the house. Undoubtedly he was working, although after last night he could be sleeping, too. There was only one way to find out. Clouds of dust puffed up from the dirt road as I braked to a halt.

I walked up his gravel driveway, climbed three rickety steps to the front porch, and knocked loudly on the door. After waiting a bit, I knocked again. No answer. I wandered about his unkempt lawn, rounded the house, and thoroughly examined the weed-ridden yard. Nowhere did I find any sign of freshly dug earth. Nothing had been buried there recently. I roved around the house trying the doors and windows. Everything was locked. Only one alternative seemed left to me.

135

But before using it, I decided to hide my car. A dense thicket about a mile away served my purpose. After my car was well camouflaged, I followed the edge of the woods back to Bodin's house.

First I checked the garage, which stood separated from the house. Its roll-down door wasn't locked. My search yielded nothing. I walked to the back of the house, found a rock among a cluster of weeds, and hurled it at one of Bodin's windows, shattering a hole in the glass. Reaching inside, I unfastened the latch and pushed the window up. Straddling the sill with one leg and grasping the sides of the window with both hands, I hauled myself into the kitchen.

The room was neither dirty nor immaculate. But its contents were old. The refrigerator was yellow and peeling. The gas range looked like an original. A jar of instant coffee had been left out on the table, and a frying pan, plate, cup, saucer, and spoon lay in the pitted porcelain sink. Beneath the sink was a metal cabinet that contained two cans of cleanser and a flit gun full of bug spray. Above the sink were a couple of built-in, walnut-stained cabinets, which contained nothing but saucers, plates, and cups.

Since the kitchen yielded no secrets, I graduated to the living room. Floral print covers were fitted over a thickly cushioned sofa and its two accompanying armchairs. A blue-glass mirror-top coffee table stood in the center of a nut-brown oval throw rug between the sofa and chairs. The rug provided the only covering for an otherwise bare plank floor. An honest-to-goodness grandfather clock ticked in one corner of the room while a stone fireplace yawned dormantly in the center of its wall. A picture of a fat couple dressed nineteen-thirties style stood framed on the fireplace mantelpiece. Both looked like Bodin. It didn't take long to investigate this room. I felt the cushions, peered under the sofa and chairs, examined the clock, and poked around the fireplace, to no avail. Next I climbed the short winding staircase to the bedrooms.

The first bedroom I entered contained an ancient brass four-poster that had been slept in and left unmade. A small mat at the side of the bed provided an inch of protection from the wood floor. A dresser, chair, and built-in closet completed the austere decor of the room. I examined everything from mattress and pillow to the pockets of his pants and jackets, and came up with a big zero. Another bedroom, decorated along the lines of this one, but dustier and unslept in, yielded nothing. The bathroom proved fruitless, and my probe of the tiny attic was a total waste of time. Only one area was left, so I went downstairs to it.

A flight of creaking wood steps led into the damp concrete basement. An old-fashioned chain-pull lightbulb, which I had no intention of using, hung from the center of the ceiling. Thankfully, enough sunlight filtered through the windows to enable me to conduct my search. The floor was concrete, none of it freshly poured. Behind the slanting staircase I noticed a hoe, two shovels, and a pick. None looked recently used. A washing machine, empty inside, and a lawn mower completed the array of objects in the basement. My disappointment barely had time to foment before I heard the noise of an engine and the crunch of gravel beneath tires.

My heart began a drum roll and my body turned slick with sweat. I looked around frantically, started toward one of the basement windows, then realized my chances of getting away in broad daylight without being spotted, and possibly shot, were nil. My only alternative was to be still and hope he didn't notice the broken window. I tiptoed quietly behind the staircase and waited.

The slam of the door upstairs was followed by the thudding of clumsy feet. Next I heard the tinkle of glass and the mouthing of colorful invectives. Inhaling deeply, I wound my fingers around the shovel, hefted it, and braced myself. The heavy tread continued above, but grew fainter as Bodin—I assumed it was he—climbed the stairs. I had tried to replace everything as I had found it so he would never realize the house had been searched and would blame the broken window on mischievous kids. Now I prayed that I had succeeded. The rapid-fire thumping of descending feet told me I'd soon find out.

The doorknob above the staircase rattled and the door squeaked open. A thin shaft of light carefully circled the basement. I held my breath and tried to integrate my bodily atoms with those of the wall. Bodin descended with deliberately measured steps. He leaned over the handrail on the side opposite to where I stood, and played the beam about. Then he crossed over to my side. I lowered the shovel until the spade hovered above my shoes. He leaned over the rail and I snapped up the shovel. The fat spade clunked against his forehead, and the stairs trembled. Perhaps the house didn't shake but I certainly did as he rolled, pistol in hand, across the concrete floor.

By the time his journey ceased, I was standing above him, ready to strike again. But that wasn't necessary. His shallow breathing and unseeing eyes told me that he'd be out for a long time. I tossed the shovel aside, climbed the steps three at a time, and peered through the living-room window as a precaution. His car, parked outside, was empty. I ran from the house to the woods like a fox from the hounds.

I returned home disappointed and shaky. I poured a double Scotch and used both hands to steady the glass as I drank. The scent of alcohol must have aroused my cat because the howl of a condemned soul was followed by the sudden appearance of a straggle-haired four-legged skeleton. He stared at my drink like a Peeping Tom at a naked girl. I said, "No good! Uh-uh! You're going to have to learn new habits. Like eating, for instance."

He cried all the way into the kitchen as though his tail were caught in a slammed door. I opened a can of tuna fish, broke it up on a paper plate, and placed it on the floor beneath his nose. He sniffed, rolled his eyes, and shook his head in what looked like disgust. When I placed a bowl of milk before him, he actually swatted my hand. But when I gently pressed his face into the tuna, he accepted the inevitable and ate. He refused, however, to even consider the milk. When he had finished off most of the tuna, I relented and poured him a beer. Before drinking it, he licked my fingers. Friends again. Now that his needs were satisfied, I returned to my thoughts.

Bodin probably knew Paradise Village better

than most housewives knew their kitchens. Undoubtedly there were innumerable hiding places for him to stash his loot. Yet, I wondered. If I had a million dollars lying about, I'd want it nearby, where someone couldn't accidentally stumble over it. But where? Pondering this thought, I downed my Scotch. Suddenly another possibility struck me. . . .

I parked outside Robin's home and walked reluctantly up to the porch. She answered my second knock. An uncertain smile played around her lips. She said, "Hello, Marty. Would you like to come in?"

She deliberately placed too much emphasis on that last word. I said, "Conversation is more or less what I had in mind."

She pouted coyly as I entered, saying, "Care for a drink?"

"Sure."

By the time Robin returned, I was comfortably settled on her couch. She handed me my drink, curled up beside me, and coddled a glass of Coke. Her eyes probed my face questioningly. I sipped my drink and said, "Excellent, Robin. You certainly have good taste."

"Are you here to flatter my taste?"

"And judgment. And intelligence. You're far more clever than I ever realized."

Aside from a barely perceptible twitch in her eyebrows, she registered no emotion. All she said was, "I don't understand."

"You will when I explain. At first I thought you liked me for myself. Later on I decided you were

140

using me to advance your own good fortune. But now . . ."

"Yes?"

"I've been adding some facts and getting some answers. I feel almost as though fate were playing tricks with my life."

"Really?"

"Do you believe in a personal, preordained destiny, Robin?"

"No."

"Neither do I—or at least I didn't—until now."

"And now you do?"

"My mind has opened up on the subject. Consider this. Either pure chance or a decision of the gods placed me in Paradise Village at this point in time, right?"

Robin shrugged. "As far as I can see, it was your own decision. Period."

"True. But no sooner had I arrived than the murders began to occur."

"Coincidence."

"Maybe. If so, it's a coincidence that must have troubled the killer."

"Why?"

"The answer's obvious. At the risk of sounding pompous, I must admit my former career speaks for itself. Now, to a clever killer, who's planned to harass a small town with an inadequate police force and an ineffectual local government, my sudden presence must have symbolized the proverbial monkey wrench."

"Haven't you overlooked something?"

I finished my drink, jiggled the ice cubes, and said, "What?"

Robin drained her soda, took my glass, and said, "Wait till I renew the drinks."

"We can talk while you're pouring."

I followed her into the kitchen and helped with the ice as she said, "How about the state police? Surely they're not ineffectual."

"They would be if the killer had an insight into their every plan."

Robin's bottle-wielding hand hesitated at right angles over my drink. I gently nudged the bottle upward. "Easy. Even my cat can't drink like that."

"Sorry—I—I'm beginning to suspect that you're talking about Sheriff Bodin."

"You're beginning to suspect right."

"That's ridiculous." Robin poured more Coke for herself. "He hasn't got the brains to dream up something like this."

"Hasn't he? I understand he was a pretty good student until he was forced to quit college."

"Really?"

"Really."

"Let's go back inside, shall we?"

"Why not?"

After we resumed sitting, Robin said, "If your facts are correct, then he's quite an actor."

"That he is."

"It—it all seems so incredible—absurd, actually."

"Why?"

"Because he—he practically forced you into joining the investigation."

"To keep an eye on me, my dear. It wouldn't quite suit his plans to have me snooping about unchecked."

Robin nodded thoughtfully and said, "I see."

142

"You should. This is where you come in."

"Me?"

Robin's teeth showed, but her eyes weren't smiling.

"Someone had to keep tabs on me," I said. "Bodin couldn't hold my hand day and night."

She frowned, blinked several times, then widened her eyes. "Surely—surely you're not suggesting. . . ." Her voice trailed off dramatically.

I said, "I'm not suggesting. I'm accusing."

"You're crazy."

"I'm logical. It adds up. How else could the tape recorder have been planted in my bungalow without a forced entry?"

"You tell me."

"The day we found Father Moore's body, you drove my car into town. I keep my bungalow and car keys together. I checked with the town's only locksmith and he told me you had a key duplicated that day."

"And you think it was yours?"

"Yes."

"They say alcohol kills brain cells, Marty. I'm beginning to believe it."

"Speaking of alcohol, I noticed you forced some down the first time we had sex but haven't drunk any since."

"What's that supposed to mean?"

"You had to use your body to keep me interested but found the thought of sex distasteful, so you bolstered your courage with Scotch."

"And I suppose you were so good I didn't need the liquor anymore, huh?"

"Exactly. Under different circumstances, I'd feel flattered."

"What a theory."

"How about this theory? A young girl is raped. Her sorrow is deepened by the loss of her father." Pink patches appeared on Robin's cheeks when I mentioned her father. "She is shamed and humiliated by the threat of being branded a whore. Even the sympathetic sheriff—a father figure, perhaps? —advises her to accept injustice. Having no other choice, she accepts. But she remembers. Oh, how she remembers!"

Robin's complexion suddenly drained and her hands shook. But her voice remained steady. She said, "I'm glad the courts convict on facts and not imagination."

"I think I know the facts. Bodin's a born loser. Bullied by the mayor. Ridiculed by the towns-people. He has his complaints and you have yours. Now, you mentioned that he used to look in on you occasionally. Sort of like a Dutch uncle. More like keeping tabs for the mayor, if you ask me."

"You do have some imagination."

"And you've got it working. On one of these visits, you pool gripes and an idea is born. Why not team up and exact some justice from the good citizens of Paradise Village?"

"Oh, Marty! Come on!"

"Whose idea was it originally, Robin? Yours or his?"

"I'm sick of this." Robin motioned toward the door. "Get out."

"Not until I've searched your place."

"You'll search nothing. I don't have to submit to this."

"We can do this the easy way or the hard way. Choose the hard way and you can always claim

144

your broken jaw was the result of a lover's quarrel."

Robin glared at me. I stood up, made a sweeping arc with my arm, and said, "Shall we commence with familiar territory? The bedroom, for instance?"

Within forty-five minutes, I had searched the house, leaving no floor mat or ice cube unturned. Robin smirked and said, "Satisfied?"

"Not quite. Let's try the garage."

"Marty, please! Let's stop this charade."

"Let's go!"

Heaving a sigh, Robin led the way. Aside from the idly squatting Bonneville, the garage was devoid of hiding places. I searched the car like a penitent sinner would his conscience, but to no avail. Finally, I crawled under it and drew another blank. Using the rear bumper and gas cap as handgrips, I hauled myself up disgustedly. Robin asked, "Now are you satisfied?"

"If you're innocent, I apologize. If not, you better burn that money because the minute you try to spend a nickel of it, you'll swing."

"Nice way to talk to a lady, Mr. Callahan."

Robin hadn't uttered those words and I don't talk to myself. Not since my divorce, anyway. Robin brushed past me as I turned to see Bodin's bulky frame. He had entered the garage from the house just as we had. A blue welt marked his forehead, and a pistol marked his fist. I said, "You recuperate quickly."

"Nothing upstairs to damage, Mr. Callahan. Or so everybody thinks."

"I didn't hear you come in," I said. "You must be pretty lightfooted for a fat man."

145

"I am when I want to be. I thought you'd be here, so I parked a few blocks away and came in without announcing myself. When I drove by last night, I saw your car here. Robin called me later and said you were getting suspicious. I'm glad she was clever enough to divert suspicion from both of us by letting it fall on me."

Robin said, "What happened to your head?"

"While I was over here with you," Bodin said, "he searched my house. Though you'd hardly know it to look at the place. Knocked me cold with a shovel when I returned."

"What are we going to do with him, Sheriff?"

"Take him for a nice drive. But first get the bottle of Scotch I saw inside. We want him relaxed and comfortable, don't we?"

Robin went into the house. I said, "This won't work. I'm too well known. There'll be investigations—"

"Sam Doddard's murder worked, and he was an influential millionaire."

"Is that why you hated him, or was it because he married the woman you wanted?"

"I had nothing against him. It was her I hated. Nose always in the air. Too good for me. She didn't look too highfalutin' at her husband's funeral or when she saw her old friend's picture, did she?"

Robin returned with the bottle. Bodin took it from her, handed it to me, and said, "Drink."

"No."

"No?"

"That's what I said. No."

"Then I'll empty this Magnum into you."

"How will you explain that to the press?"

"Easy. Everyone knows you and Robin have

been seein' each other. She decided to break off with you, and you threatened her. I stopped by to see how she was after yesterday's ordeal and caught you slappin' her around—"

"She hasn't a mark on her, Sheriff."

"She will have, Mr. Callahan. Then you struck me in the head." Bodin pointed to his welt. "And I shot you."

"Do you really think the people will buy this story?"

"They'll accept it from Robin. She is the local heroine, you know. Now drink."

Bodin cocked his pistol and I raised the bottle to my lips.

"Robin," he said, "soon's it's dark, we're going for a drive in Mr. Callahan's car to that spot we talked about."

Robin's eyes avoided mine. She said, "The cliff . . ."

"Right. It's perfect. He drove drunk down a deserted back road. Didn't know the area. Foolproof."

"I had hoped it wouldn't come to this, Sheriff," she said. "He didn't commit crimes against us like—"

"Nonsense! He's just as much a part of *them* as the mayor or anybody else. Understand me?"

"Yes." Robin's eyes became polished green pebbles. "Marty's got to go."

"Cheers," I said.

I had a bellyful of booze by the time we started out, but I've always been able to hold quite a bit and wasn't as drunk as I seemed. Robin drove and Bodin sat beside her while I slumped in the back

147

seat, staring down the bore of his gun. He said, "When it's over, Robin, you stay calm. Just walk home through the woods as nonchalantly as you would any other time. I'll take another route back to my car. Eventually, when the wreck is found, you just say he got drunk, became stubborn, and insisted on driving home. The autopsy will bear you out."

"Very shmart," I said. "You two will fosh—fox —yourselves into the pen. Mark my words."

"Listen to the hotshot detective, Robin. Smart as he's supposed to be, he didn't find the money, did he?"

"No."

"See? He's not so smart after all."

"I'm shmart enough to know you killed Robinsh father." I was deliberately slurring my speech.

The car swerved slightly as Robin's eyes flashed from the road to the rearview mirror. Bodin's gun hand coordinated perfectly with the sudden movement, never losing its target. Robin said, "What are you talking about, Marty?"

"Ignore him," Bodin interrupted. "He's conning you. Trying to save his hide."

"Can you ignore thish, Robin? Bodin would sh—still be a car mechanic if it wasn't for Mayor Hanlon—hic—right? Now—"

"Shut up, Callahan!"

"Why? If itsh—it's only a con, I mean?"

"Let Marty talk, Sheriff."

"Look, Robin—"

"No!" I said. "Listen, Robin. Your father's death was no accident. It was a well-executed murder. Here's the facts—"

148

"Callahan, shut your mouth or I'll put a bullet into it."

"Ask him why he wants me to shut up, Robin. Ask him!"

"Let him talk, Sheriff. I mean it!"

"Callahan's a phony, Robin. He's not even that drunk. Notice he stopped slurring his words? He's trying to divide us—"

"Think, Robin," I said. "Bodin's always been the mayor's flunky. All those times he's looked in on you, sympathized with you, he was spying for his boss."

Again the car swerved. Bodin said, "He's lying. I hate the mayor and this town as much as you do. That's why—when we came up with this idea—I asked you to be my partner."

"More lies, Robin," I said. "Once the idea was born between you, Bodin realized he could make it work, but you'd know who was behind it, so he had to take you into his scheme."

Robin's driving grew steadier. She said, "Marty, I don't believe you. He didn't need me as a partner. He wanted me. I could have been one of his victims and no one would have been the wiser."

"Yes, but not the first victim. The first had to be someone prominent to really impress the town. I think you would have been a victim if I hadn't come along. But with me here he found a better use for you. You could spy on me for him like he spied on you for Mayor Hanlon. You could tell him what I was thinking and influence my actions just as he saw to it that you acted in a way that suited his boss."

"Callahan," Bodin growled, "shut up or I'll waste you right now!"

"Killed by you in my own car? That'd be tough to explain. Besides, I haven't told Robin the best part yet. I'm sure she wants to hear it."

"Goddamn you—" Bodin raised his gun to strike me.

"Sheriff!" Robin's harsh tone made him hesitate. "Let him finish."

"Robin," I said, "your father was an embarrassment to the mayor. Bodin, an ex-mechanic, fixed your father's car so it would crash. He probably did it while your father and you were in the hospital."

Robin's knuckles whitened on the steering wheel. Her foot was heavy on the accelerator. She threw a stony glance toward Bodin, who said, "Jesus! Watch the road!"

"Ask him why he examined the wreck personally instead of allowing Doddard's mechanic to do the job as usual."

"I can explain that," Bodin said. "It—the mayor thought I'd—uh—I was a better mechanic. I'd do a better job—"

"Exactly, Robin. Your father's murderer would do a better job!"

Robin floored the brake, tires screeched, and the earth seemed to reverse in its rotation. I vaulted over the front seat and caught Bodin's gun hand with both of mine just as the world spun completely out of orbit. A thunderclap rocked my brain, and fire seared my face. Flesh slapped flesh and bone struck bone as the topsy-turvy motion of the car ended with a jolt. Robin's dazed form was draped over my sore body. I moved her head gently aside with my cheek and looked up at the floor and seat. Wedged sideways between

150

the dashboard and front seat, Bodin seemed to be standing on the blood clot that was once his head. I didn't see the gun. Robin blinked and moaned. As the glaze disappeared from her eyes, she said, "What—what happened?"

"We've turned upside down. Can you reach the door handle?"

"I—I think—oh, wow!"

"Don't look at him!" I raised a slightly numb arm and nudged her face away from Bodin's direction. I didn't want her puking all over me. "Open the door."

Robin grasped the handle, tugged futilely, and said, "I can't. It won't budge."

"We're upside down. Try the other way."

She did and the lock clicked. After a few combined thrusts, we worked the door open against the resistance of a thick bush. I let her crawl out over me, then followed. I crawled through the thicket and finally ended upright on wobbly legs. Robin looked much sturdier than I felt, standing in the moonlight with Bodin's pistol in her hand. We were near the bottom of a nine-foot ravine. Below us my car lay upside down like a huge dead bug.

"Thanks for removing the sheriff," she said. "Makes for a better end to this story."

A flashlight suddenly glowed from above. I glanced upward, laughed, and said, "Shoot me and it'll end with a twist."

Robin's eyes darted toward the shadowy figure descending toward us. I recognized the deputy named Dick. He hollered, "You people all right?"

"Just dandy," I answered.

"I've been cruising around, looking for the sheriff," he said. "Saw you go over the. . . ."

Dick's voice faded when he saw the gun in Robin's hand. He frowned, then said, "What the hell's going on?"

"Arrest Callahan," she answered. "He murdered Sheriff Bodin."

"Murdered? The sheriff?"

"His body's in the car. Callahan shot him with this gun. We crashed. I climbed out of the car and found the gun on the ground. Callahan would have killed me, too. He—"

Dick's brow wrinkled. He said, "Is this true, Mr. Callahan?"

"Partially."

"Did you shoot the sheriff?"

"Yes. In a way."

Robin began to perspire, even though it was a cool evening. The gun began to shake in her hand. I said, "Dick, take that gun before I get shot, will you?"

He held his own pistol while slipping a pencil through the trigger guard of Bodin's gun to avoid smudging any fingerprints. Robin said, "Callahan thought the sheriff and I took the ransom, that we engineered the plot to kill those people. He broke into the sheriff's house looking for the money. . . . The sheriff came home unexpectedly. . . . Callahan knocked him out . . . came after me . . . searched my house. . . . Bodin woke up . . . came to my place. . . ."

"Easy, Robin," I said. "You've got a good story. Don't run out of breath now."

"The sheriff didn't find Callahan home . . . he knew we were dating . . . so he came to my place

. . . arrested him. But Marty jumped him and took the gun. He forced us to drive back to the sheriff's house, where he still believed the money to be. Bodin tried to disarm him. God! It was awful!"

I clapped and said, "Bravo!"

Robin's voice grew shrill as she said, "He even accused Bodin of killing my father under Mayor Hanlon's orders!"

Dick's eyebrows climbed. He said, "Is that true?"

"Yes," I said. "That's true."

"You must be crackers. I'm bringing you both in. I have to view the sheriff's body, but first I'm going to secure you, Mr. Callahan."

Robin smirked. I extended my hands and said, "Bracelets, please."

Chapter Twelve

This vacation was such that finishing it in jail seemed almost proper. Instead of a mere sheriff as my companion, I had Robin, the recently returned mayor, the whole police force, and a battery of news reporters. Not to mention the fact that most of the town was gathered outside. I refused to listen to the *Miranda* speech and rejected my right to a lawyer, but insisted on making a public statement when Robin finished her monologue. Ladies first, of course. TV cameras whirred, flashbulbs popped, and pens scratched on pads throughout the session. The public was not allowed in or out—with one exception.

Mrs. Doddard.

Attired in a knee-length black dress, she floated past the police and reporters, ignoring all questions leveled at her. Robin looked annoyed as attention was diverted from her. A sea of flashing bulbs bathed us as Mrs. Doddard placed her hand in mine and said, "News of this absurd accusation was on the radio. I came as quickly as I could."

"Believe me"—I squeezed her hand—"I appreciate your concern."

"Have you a lawyer?"

"Don't need one. I'll end this circus in a jiffy."

Silence struck suddenly, as though a sound-proof door had been slammed on a noisy party. I said, "Ladies and gentlemen and"—I turned my gaze toward Robin—"monsters. You've heard all the facts tonight, though in a somewhat biased fashion. Now, let me give you my beliefs and my facts. I believe Mayor Hanlon ordered Robin's father killed to save his son from being charged with, and himself embarrassed by, a case of rape."

"Mr. Callahan—" Either the mayor's chest swelled under his pin-striped suit or he was wearing a blowfish for a necktie. "I will not be scandalized by—"

"Shut up!" My bark canceled his speech and deflated his chest. I continued, "It is my contention that he ordered Bodin, his number-one flunky, who happened to be a car mechanic, to fix Mr. Blair's car to crash. Mrs. Doddard here"—all eyes fastened upon her—"can testify to the fact that Bodin personally examined the car after the accident, breaking the established precedent of having all wrecks examined at her husband's garage."

"Is that true, Mr. Mayor?" asked Aaron Farmer.

"I—well—" The mayor's facial pores had become geysers of sweat.

"It's true," chimed my elegant ally.

"So?" the mayor piped up. "He was a good mechanic, right?"

"That he was," I said. "And since Robin insisted on keeping her father's car, we can have another good mechanic reexamine it."

"So have it examined," the mayor said. "We—

155

we want the truth to come out. But—even if it was fixed—Bodin did it on his own. My hands are clean."

Mayor Hanlon actually held his hands up to the cameras. He had a lovely manicure. Robin said, "Why is everyone listening to Marty? He's a murderer. He admitted murdering the sheriff right in front of Dick, one of your own deputies."

The mayor's little head swiveled toward the deputy. "Did he actually admit that, Dick?"

"Almost."

"Almost?" Robin and the mayor spoke simultaneously.

"Programmed by the same computer?" I asked.

Dick said, "Mr. Callahan said he shot the sheriff 'in a way.' He didn't use the word *murder*."

"'In a way'?" asked the mayor. "What's that mean?"

"That means," I said, "that he was taking me for a ride. I had broken into his house and searched it, to no avail. Just as Robin said. He returned home and I bopped him. I figured if he didn't have the dough, Robin did. I was searching her house when he showed up. He was taking me for what was to be a fatal accident, when I enraged Robin, who happened to be driving, by telling her the truth about her father's death. She hit the brake, and I went for his gun. It discharged, as the burn on my face clearly indicates, and he was killed."

Aaron Farmer asked, "What made you suspect Robin and the sheriff?"

"Many things. But mainly the fact that together they had the best access to the money."

"Lies!" Green flames danced in Robin's eyes as

they bored into mine. "Remember the night Captain Edison prepared his trap? The sheriff and I were both present when the killer phoned. How could we be guilty? Or—or are you going to accuse us of having a third accomplice, Mr. Detective?"

"You had a third, all right. But he was an unwitting accomplice. I can't prove it, but I believe the sheriff paid Charley Fetters to make that phone call at the appointed time without really telling him why. Charley's finances had zoomed upward about this time, and he wasn't the type to question such sudden good fortune."

"Rubbish!" Robin snarled. "If this nonsense were really true, then how come you haven't found the money?"

I tapped my forehead with my forefinger and said, "Oh, but I have."

Silence formed a vacuum about us. I said, "The first time I saw your father's car, the gas cap was missing."

"Gas cap?" Fear melted the hardness in Robin's eyes. "I—I don't—know what you're—"

"Bodin's remark about my not finding the money made me realize I had overlooked something. Thinking back, I remembered hoisting myself up from under the car with the aid of the bumper and gas cap. I think if you policemen will check that tank, you'll find it filled with something more precious than gasoline."

Chapter Thirteen

I was packing to leave this so-called Paradise with the enthusiasm of a lifer who's suddenly been paroled. Maybe back in New York City I could get some writing done. My cat, though uncertain, I'm sure, of the occasion, was merrily lapping up a can of beer, when a knock came at my door. It was a gentle, feminine rapping, such as the kind that had led me to open the door to this whole misadventure. I hesitated, but the tapping persisted. So, bracing myself, I swung the door open. Mrs. Doddard smiled beneath her wire-framed sunglasses and said, "Hello, Mr. Callahan. May I come in?"

"By all means, do." As she entered, I saw her chauffeur-occupied Rolls outside. "Care for a drink?"

"Scotch and water will be fine."

"Ice?"

"Please."

I ushered her to the sofa and said, "Back in a sec."

Returning with two drinks, I handed her one, sat beside her, and said, "Cheers."

We clinked glasses and drank. A moment of

thoughtful silence elapsed before she spoke. "Packing, I see."

"Figure I better end this vacation before it ends me."

"It has been unique, hasn't it?"

"I'll say. Anyhow, now that the money's been recovered and Robin's confessed, there's no reason for me to stay anymore."

"What about remaining to have a real vacation?"

"No, thanks. I'm kind of soured on this place."

"I'm sorry to hear that. What about him?"

She nodded toward Obnoxious, who was stretched out sideways, taut as a guitar string. I said, "He'll love New York. Plenty of beer there."

Mrs. Doddard laughed and said, "Do you think you'll ever come back?"

"I doubt it."

"Too bad. You could go far here. Probably become mayor if you wanted to."

"I suppose I could. Especially if Hanlon runs again."

"He wouldn't dare. Not since my mechanics have proved Robin's father's brake linings had been tampered with."

"That did lend credence to my theory, didn't it?"

"Enough to convict the mayor in the eyes of the voters, if not the law."

"How is your mechanic, by the way? The one I met when—uh—"

"Fine. He's an apprentice, actually. He thinks highly of you. It's his idea that you should run for mayor."

"Tell him I said no thanks. I'm not interested in politics."

"I—I guess this—experience has caused you to lose interest in us completely, hasn't it?"

"Not completely, no."

A spark seemed to flicker in her eyes as she said, "Oh?"

"I feel a very strong interest in a certain lovely lady."

"Thank you. I appreciate that, but—I—I—loved my husband very much, and. . . ."

"I know."

"He's—gone so short a time. . . ."

I placed my hand over hers and said, "I understand. There's no need—"

"Yes, there is, Marty." Her use of my first name exhilarated me. I hadn't felt like this since I shared my gumdrops with Susan Macintosh in the seventh grade. She continued, "Perhaps—some-day—you could come back again for a visit. Sometime in the future, when the wounds have healed all around."

"It's certainly something to think about, Mrs. Doddard."

"Violet."

"Violet."

Violet Doddard stood up, kissed my cheek, and left. I watched her car disappear down the road, then I closed the door and nearly tripped over my snoring cat. I laughed, realizing that while my future might be uncertain, one thing was for sure.

I had found myself a loyal drinking partner.

0-595-20056-7

Made in United States
North Haven, CT
25 March 2022

17518090R00100